DARK

EERIE RIVER PUBLISHING

DARK MAGIC
DRABBLES OF MAGIC AND LORE

Copyright © 2021 Eerie River Publishing
All Rights Reserved.

This book is a work of fiction.
Names, characters, places, events, organizations and incidents are either part of the author's imagination or are used fictitiously. Except the monsters, those are real.

No part of this book may be reproduced in any manner, or transmitted in any form or by any means, electronic, mechanical, photocopying, recording or otherwise, without express written permission by the author(s) and or publisher.

Paperback ISBN: 978-1-990245-14-5
Hardcover ISBN: 978-1-990245-15-2
Digital ISBN: 978-1-990245-05-3

Edited by Alanna Robertson-Webb
Cover design Michelle River
Book Formatting by Michelle River

**ALSO AVAILABLE FROM
EERIE RIVER PUBLISHING**

NOVELS
STORMING AREA 51

HORROR ANTHOLOGIES

Don't Look: 12 Stories of Bite Sized Horror
It Calls From The Forest: Volume I
It Calls From The Forest: Volume II
It Calls From The Sky
Darkness Reclaimed
Midnight Shadow: Volume I

DARK FANTASY ANTHOLOGIES
With Blood and Ash
With Bone and Iron

DRABBLE COLLECTIONS
Forgotten Ones: Drabbles of Myth and Legend

COMING SOON
It Calls From The Sea
It Calls From the Doors
It Calls From the Veil
The Sentinel
In Solitude's Shadow
The Void
A Sword Named Sorrow
AFTER: A Post Apocalyptic Series

This book is dedicated to our families and friends, to those who have stood by us, coffee in hand, and told us never to give up on our dreams.

In these strange times we would also like to dedicate this book to the front-line workers that fight to keep us all safe, to the parents that had to make the hard decision to stay home and the unseen and overlooked heros who make our lives possible. Thank you.

STORIES & AUTHORS

SACRED GROUND 17
WHICH JAR? 18
THE COURTYARD 19
THE ASCENT................................... 20
BEDTIME STORIES 21
   B.K. BASS................................... 22
APEP OF EGYPT................................ 23
   ALANNA ROBERTSON-WEBB 24
AMUSE-BOUCHE............................... 25
SWEET TOOTH................................. 26
LITTLE FLYING FLESH-EATERS.................. 27
SLEEP! THE TOOTH FAIRY'S COMING............. 28
THE ELVES AND THE SHOEMAKER 29
   CALLUM PEARCE 30
UNGRATEFUL 31
SIXTH MISTAKE 32
HEARTSTRUCK................................. 33
BLOOD LETTER................................ 34
ONE SHADOW 35
   WILLIAM A. WELLMAN........................ 36
THE SLEEP FARM 37
THE LAST LULLABY 38
ETERNAL DARKNESS 39
TO RAISE THE DEAD 40
SHADOWS OF THE EARTH 41
   MCKENZIE RICHARDSON 42
THE CELLAR 43
   MICHELLE BRYAN 44

HAPPPILY EVER AFTER	45
FOR WHOM THE BELL TOLLS	46
THE DANCE	47
K.G. LEWIS	48
RETURN POLICY	49
BAD DRUGS	50
SUMMER READING	51
DUSTIN WALKER	52
THE QUILL WITCH	53
E. JOAN ARMSTRONG	54
THE BASILISK OF BARNABAS BRIMSTONE	55
THE VISITOR	56
THE WATER HORSE	57
THE CURIOUS CASE OF CASSEY COULTER	58
SANDY BUTCHERS	59
A MASS GRAVE	60
PAUL BENKENDORFER	61
A TECHNICALITY	62
A SORCERER'S LAMENT	63
JUST A LITTLE COMPANY	64
FRIENDS IN HIGH PLACES	65
NOBLE PROBLEMS	66
PETER VANGELDEREN	67
THE VIOLINIST	68
THE NORTHERN COLD	69
B.B. BLAZKOWICZ	70
HE AWAKENS	71
ADRIAN J. JOHNSON	72
TEACH THEM TERROR	73
PRISONER	74
FIREFLIES	75
THE PRICE	76
UNTIL DAWN	77

WHISPERS	78
CONSTANTINE E. KIOUSIS	79
THROWING THE BONES	80
INSCRIBED	81
FOREWARNED	82
BENEATH THE SKIN	83
MARY RAJOTTE	84
DUMPED	85
BELINDA BRADY	86
EVOCATION	87
FAILURE	88
CITY DEFENDER	89
PATRONAGE REVOKED	90
HIGHWAY ROBBERY	91
DAMIEN ALLMARK	92
SHIPWRECKED	93
DANCE OF THE DRYAD	94
DEADLY LEGENDS	95
BENEATH THE SURFACE	96
DARLENE HOLT	97
RISE AND FALL	98
LAURAINE S BLAKE	99
THE DESTROYER	100
THE GARDEN OF LOST SOULS	101
THE HUNT	102
A TASTE OF MURDER	103
CHARLOTTE LANGTREE	104
THE REAPER	105
THE IMPORTANCE OF SILENCE	106
IT LURKS BENEATH	107
DIANA ALLGAIR	108
BONES, THEN HORNS, THEN UDDERS	109
BONES, THEN TEETH, THEN WINGS	110

B. J. THROWER 111
WHITE CAT 112
   THOMAS STURGEON JR 113
THE SECOND WAVE 114
DISCOVERED 115
SACRIFICE 116
   NERISHA KEMRAJ 117
BLOOD-RED LIPS 118
   SHELDON WOODBURY 119
MAVEN'S ARROW 120
FOREVER MINE 121
DESPERATE 122
   A.S. MACKENZIE 123
THE ARCANE AMATEUR 124
RESURRECTION MEN 125
TEARS FOR THE DEAD 126
NEVER LOOK AT ITS FACE 127
   TERRENCE MCKINNIES 128
A PROMISE KEPT 129
DADDY'S LITTLE GIRL 130
   PETER ANDREW SMITH 131
LONGEVITY 132
THE DEAD ROOM 133
   CHRIS LILIENTHAL 134
THE PAIN OF VENGEANCE 135
WAS IT WORTH IT? 136
THRICE TO THINE AND THRICE TO MINE 137
   K.B. ELIJAH 138
THE SHADOW 139
   CHRISSIE ROHRMAN 140
THE SIREN'S SYMPHONY 141
   EZ WHITNEY 142
CLOCKMAKER'S CURSE 143

CONCRETE CERTAINTY	144
N.M. BROWN	145
NOT A WITCH	146
A.E. HELLSTORM	147
BRACKISH MISTAKES	148
SHERRY OSBORNE	149
THE ALICANTO WILL FLY AGAIN	150
THREE THREE THREE	151
KAIDA STEALS THE SHOW	152
XIMENA ESCOBAR	153
INFERNO TEMPEST	154
G.L. DALTON	155
KIRIGAMI	156
PIANZI (IMPOSTOR)	157
FRANCES LU-PAI IPPOLITO	158
MALPHA	159
D'MITRI BLACKWOOD	160
BURNING ANGER	161
THE SORCERESS	162
CLIMAX	163
COMING OF AGE	164
THE WAND	165
CHISTO HEALY	166
AMBITION	167
RICH RURSHELL	168
A DEBT	169
FRIENDS IN OTHER PLACES	170
SOPHIE WAGNER	171
CHANGES	172
KATIE JORDAN	173
THE LAST KING	174
CURTIS A. DEETER	175
AVIARY	176

OF SMOKE AND SHADOW	177
SACRAMENT	178
BURNING MAN	179
THE DEVIL'S WORK	180
MARC SORONDO	181
THE CITADEL	182
JACEK WILKOS	183
THE HELL HOUND COMETH	184
GORDON DUNLEAVY	185
THE EARLY BIRD CATCHES THE WYRM	186
CHRISTIAN BOUSTEAD	187
BLOOD MAGIC	188
TOO MUCH	189
A MATTER OF CONCENTRATION	190
THEIR GOD'S REBIRTH	191
STOLEN GOODS	192
DAVID GREEN	193
BOOKWORM	194
FIRST BORN	195
LAURENCE SULLIVAN	196
SOLUTION-ORIENTED	197
CAUGHT BETWEEN	198
THE MUSIC OF LIFE	199
ON THE NIGHT OF THE FIFTH MOON	200
KIMBERLY REI	201
FULL-MOON VENGEANCE	202
FAMILY SECRETS	203
A DIFFERENT KIND OF GENIE	204
NICOLE HONL	205
WRATHFUL AS ROSES	206
IGNATIO'S CALLING	207
THE AUDITION	208
THE SACRIFICE'S REVENGE	209

THE UN-FAMILIAR 210
   SARAH MATTHEWS 211
THE UNQUIET DEAD 212
THE WITCH'S DANCE 213
THE OLD ONES 214
   J. A. SKELTON 215
GONE WITH THE WAVES 216
LYPHUS' ARMY 217
ARMORED PROTECTOR 218
OZILDOR'S RETRIBUTION 219
AZOTHOR'S NEW SPELL 220
   RADAR DEBOARD 221
THE PROOF 222
THE WILL OF THE STORM 223
NO SECOND CHANCES 224
   CLINT FOSTER 225
ESCAPE 226
THE WARLOCKS CHARGE 227
DEATH OF THE QUEEN 228
THE RITE 229
THE FAMILIAR 230
   MICHAEL D. NADEAU 231
LA VENGANZA 232
FEW RETURN 233
   C. MARRY HULTMAN 234
VENGEANCE 235
   AL PROVANCE 236
MORRIGAN'S GIFT 237
WOOD WITCH 238
   R. S. PYNE 239
FORBIDDEN POWERS 240
   LAUREN RAYBOULD 241
ASHES OF THE GRIMOIRE 242

THE GIRL STEPPED AWAY FROM THE WINDOW . . . 243
   WARREN BENEDETTO 244
EMPTY AND DRAWN 245
MORE THAN DUST 246
MURMURATIONS 247
   R. H. NEWFIELD 248
COMMUTED SENTENCE 249
BLOOD BIRD 250
THIRST. 251
   PETER J. FOOTE 252
HAG-RIDDEN 253
   J. DAVID REED 254
ANOTHER EXECUTION 255
HEARTS OF STONE 256
   JACQUELINE MORAN MEYER 257
HER BLACK WINGS 258
   JOSHUA E. BORGMANN 259
LAST LETTER. 260
   DANIEL LORING KEATING 261
AN OFFERING 262
THE BLACK FLAMES 263
MOTHER DEAREST 264
   SCOTT MCGREGOR 265
A PRICE FOR DEATH 266
   AMBER M. SIMPSON 267
DAMBALLA 268
JACK O' LANTERN 269
LAST WORDS 270
THE APPLE THIEF 271
LAST STATEMENT OF A GRAVE ROBBER 272
   LAMONT A. TURNER 273
A STROLL DOWN MEMORY LANE 274
   ALEX AZAR 275

ZOMBIELAND WALDEN	276
HENRY HERZ	277
SIGHTLESS	278
TRUE LOVE'S LAST KISS	279
DEREK DUNN	280
DISAPPEARANCE TO THE DARK REALM	281
JOHN CADY	282
KULILU	283
POPPET	284
HOLLEY CORNETTO	285
EYE ON THE PRIZE	286
LIFE'S TOIL	287
J.W. GARRETT	288
THE HANGED WOMAN	289
LUCY ROSE	290
CELEBRATION	291
HELL BROTH	292
EMMA K. LEADLEY	293
THE FORBIDDEN ARTS	294
THE FINAL WAR	295
FIRE AND MADNESS	296
DALE PARNELL	297
THE WITCH'S TREE	298
JOSH GRANT-YOUNG	299
IT'S NOT	300
DOWN IN THE DEEP DARK	301
FAERIE FRUIT	302
AND THE PRINCE GAVE CHASE	303
GEORGIA COOK	304
ASH AND WING	305
S.N. GRAVES	306
THE QUEEN`S DEBT	307
MARSHA WEBB	308

THE LAST DRAGON'S SACRIFICE	309
THE HALFING-CHILD'S REVENGE	310
THE ARCHANGEL OF GRIEF	311
CURSE OF THE NEKOMATA	312
I AM THE KOLM	313
LYNDSEY ELLIS-HOLLOWAY	314
CURRENTS	315
BAUBLE	316
A REAL PAGE-TURNER	317
SONYA LAWSON	318
THE DATE	319
THE TUTOR	320
SPENCER HELSEL	321
LENTEN LAMENT OF THE ROUGAROU	322
EN-NADDĀHA	323
NICK WILKINSON	324
SUMMONING A DEMON	325
THEY BEG FOR MERCY	326
WHAT MERCY DEATH WOULD BE	327
FAIRY LIGHTS	328
NEEN COHEN	329
WIELDING THE UNEXPECTED	330
WRATH OF ICE	331
CHEQUES AND BALANCES	332
FOUNTAIN OF YOUTH	333
TREE OF KNOWLEDGE	334
FLESH OF MY FLESH	335
FORBIDDEN FRUIT	336
K.T. TATE	337
THE COST	338
THE LAST WITCH	339
THE BATTLE FOR THE SKIES	340
DIY BLACK MAGIC	341

RECESSION.	342
L. T. EMERY	343
TO FEEL MORE ALIVE	344
KAITLYN ARNETT	345
THE BARD'S ARROW	346
THE FALL OF POMPEI	347
A CROWN'S WEIGHT	348
KRIS KINSELLA	349
THAT LADY BLUE	350
THE KNIGHT	351
THE BABY OF THE FAMILY	352
SAVAGERY	353
DEAD MEN'S TALES	354
CHRIS BANNOR	355
BLOOD IS THE LIFE	356
DEEP IN THE WOODS	357
ELIZABETH DAVIS	358
EARTHBOUND	359
HER ETERNAL REWARD	360
DORMANT	361
HEAR THE OCEAN	362
S.O. GREEN	363
AMBITION	364
PURPOSE	365
TRADITION	366
T.M. BROWN	367
HIDE AND FREAK	368
THE BURNING	369
BLOODY SUMMONERS!	370
I'LL DIE ON THAT HILL	371
SEEN, BUT NOT HEARD	372
CHRIS HEWITT	373

Sacred Ground
(The Shadowspire Chronicle: 1 of 5)
B.K. Bass

A tower was being built on Beggar's Square. A shanty town once stood there, until a fire wiped it away—along with every soul trapped in the ramshackle hovels.

"Cursed ground, they say," Doran muttered as he heaved a granite block atop a newly-risen wall.

He glanced up to find a pair of disembodied, glowing eyes looking back at him. Translucent hands grasped the block. Laughter echoed through Doran's mind.

He suddenly felt his grip slacken.

The monolithic stone wavered, tilted and fell.

The stonemason's screams were cut short as his ribcage was shattered and his torso crushed to pulp.

Which Jar?

(The Shadowspire Chronicle: 2 of 5)
B.K. Bass

Malachanezer's quill scratched across parchment as he bent over the dusty, cluttered desk.

"This one?"

"No."

"This?"

"No." He shook his head in dismay at his inept, young apprentice.

"This?" Vaelish held up a jar filled with a viscous, green substance.

"By the gods, no!" Malachenezer yelled.

Vaelish, startled, dropped the vessel.

Glass shards danced across the granite floor. Viridescent mists coiled about the apprentice as blood welled from his eyes, nose and mouth.

The wizard shot to his feet, toppling ink over the parchment which mirrored the blood pooling at Vaelish's feet.

Dark, malevolent laughter echoed through the tower.

The Courtyard
(The Shadowspire Chronicle: 3 of 5)
B.K. Bass

Eckhart stumbled over the rough cobbles, turning the wine jug up only to find it empty. He dropped it and wavered, catching himself on an iron gate which swung open with a tortured groan.

He stumbled into a courtyard, where dead brambles writhed in the shadow of a tower.

A green mist flowed about Eckhart's ankles. He felt himself urged closer to the spire, prickling sensations running across his skin.

He looked down to find blood oozing from every pore.

"Wha—"

His panicked words were choked off as noxious mist flowed into his throat.

Laughter echoed through the night.

The Ascent
(The Shadowspire Chronicle: 4 of 5)
B.K. Bass

Wren spun around, sure he'd heard scratching along the stairs spiraling into the darkness below. Nothing. He leaned back and sighed.

Turning back to the granite steps before him he continued his ascent of the Shadowspire—a torch held ahead and a dagger clenched in a white-knuckled grip.

He took one step.

Deep laughter coiled dread about Wren's heart a moment before long, sharp talons raked through his flesh. They slashed out from a verdant haze as two glowing eyes locked on his.

Wren's dagger clattered on the bloody steps and the torchlight dwindled, then disappeared into the void below.

Bedtime Stories

(The Shadowspire Chronicle: 5 of 5)
B.K. Bass

"And none have ever returned from the Shadowspire."

"Are the stories true, Mum?" Thomas asked.

Isabelle smiled at her boy. "Oh, I'm sure they are."

Thomas peered out his bedroom window into the darkness.

"Fret not, my love." Isabelle snuffed out the candle, kissed Thomas goodnight and closed his door behind her.

Thomas thought he heard someone laughing outside. He threw back his blanket and crawled to the window.

Glowing eyes met his as he peered out.

"You'll help, won't you?" A deep voice rumbled. "You'll help me..."

"...kill them all," Thomas said as a verdant gleam lit his eyes.

B.K. Bass

B.K. Bass is the author of over a dozen works of science fiction, fantasy, and horror inspired by the pulp fiction magazines of the early 20th century and classic speculative fiction. He is a student of history with a particular focus on the ancient, classical, and medieval eras. He has a lifetime of experience with a specialization in business management and human relations and served in the U.S. Army. B.K. is also the Senior Writing Director for Worldbuilding Magazine.

https://bkbass.com https://twitter.com/B_K_Bass

Apep of Egypt
Alanna Robertson-Webb

"Not good enough!"

His kopesh slices punishingly against my face, the sword splitting my flesh open.

I lick my abused lips, the blood a familiar burn in my throat. I try to speak, but my broken mouth flops uselessly.

"Now, little worm, do you remember how to worship your true god?"

Snakes birthed from corrupt, sickly-green magic twine up my legs, their scales scraping chunks from my skin. I nod frantically, desperate to keep them from reaching my neck, but I am too late.

As my eyes bulge, the god's magic seeping into my veins, he laughs.

It is beautiful.

Alanna Robertson-Webb

Alanna Robertson-Webb is an author and editor who enjoys long weekends of LARPing, is terrified of sharks and finds immense fun in being the editor-in-chief at Eerie River Publishing. She one day aspires to run her own nerd-themed restaurant, as well as her own LARP game.

She has edited over ten books, such as Infected by Blair Daniels, A Cure for Chaos: Horror Stories from Hospitals and Psych Wards by Haunted House Publishing, The Deliverer by Tara Devlin and all of the current Eerie River Publishing anthologies. Alanna's writing has been published in over ninety different collections, and her work can be found at:

https://arwauthor.wixsite.com/arwauthor and at amazon.com/author/alannarobertsonwebb.

Amuse-Bouche
Callum Pearce

Each witch had to give a little blood, then the ritual would be complete. The dark lord would return to the land. How he'd thank them, these clever women, for working those spells and releasing him from his prison below.

Adding the final ingredients to the bowl blood and herbs bubbled and boiled. Soon it spilled like tar, the fallen angel clawing his way out where the mixture had fallen. Then each got a taste of the Devil's gratitude. He ripped their hearts from their chests, hungrily sucking them dry. The blood from the ritual was a marvellous appetizer.

Sweet Tooth
Callum Pearce

Gingerbread walls, candy-cane decorations and giant cupcakes scattered around the edible garden. Of course it was too good to be true, of course it must be a trap. Little Robert's eyes were bigger than the sugar glass windows.

He could just nibble around the edges, he didn't have to cross the fence. Sadly, it never works out perfectly for sweet-toothed little boys. Once they start they can't stop until their belly is swollen and aching. He chomped a path to the waiting witch. Arriving full of sugar, he soon found out that witches have a sweet tooth too.

Little Flying Flesh-Eaters
Callum Pearce

CLAP!

"Got you, little shit!"

People thought fairies were cute, but Jeff saw them for what they were: bloodthirsty, vicious monsters. He didn't see the giant swarm that the smear in his hands had strayed from.

In seconds they covered every inch of his body. They chewed off chunks of his flesh, like cookie-cutter sharks in a feeding-frenzy. Running and screaming, Jeff waved his arms redundantly, uselessly. When the swarm had you it kept you until nothing remained. Blood gushed from the expanding wounds. His body gave up as the fairies dug deeper, intent on devouring his organs.

Sleep! The Tooth Fairy's Coming
Callum Pearce

Sam heard the clicking as the fairy crept up the stairs. With every step a hundred tiny clicks. Sleep before the tooth fairy comes, they had warned. This made Sam more curious.

He had always wondered why she refused to be seen, so tonight he stayed alert. The clicking got closer, his bravery departing.

He quivered under the quilt.

The door creaked open; the covers pulled back. Sam screamed as the salivating, hideous, sharp-toothed creature leaned over him. He'd heard of the clicking cloak made of collected teeth, but nobody had mentioned the armor made of curious children's bones.

The Elves and the Shoemaker
Callum Pearce

He felt guilty watching the elves working hard to make shoes, but with his wife and son dying he needed all of the profits they could make. Bread and water was all he could pay.

That night the elves crept into the house with another payment in mind. They punctured the bodies of the shoemaker's family, collecting the blood that spilled out into bottles. They hungrily lapped and sucked at the wounds as soon as their receptacles were filled. The bottles were fed to the corpse of their queen, whose reanimation would ensure enough human blood for them all.

Callum Pearce

Callum Pearce is a Dutch storyteller, originally from Liverpool. He is a fiction writer published multiple times across a variety of platforms. A Lover of the magical as well as the macabre. He lives in a foggy old fishing town in the Netherlands with his husband and a couple of cat shaped sprites. Popping up in all of the best drabble collections and anthologies or online.

www.twitter.com/Aladdinsane79
www.facebook.com/calmpeace13

Ungrateful
William A. Wellman

I sleep in darkness, dreaming of the daylight. I feel I have grown old here, imprisoned and alone. A noise stirs me—can it be? Has someone come to find me? They are calling my name. They want me; they remembered. I rise to find my chains are broken.

I go crawling through the shadows to meet them. They stand with wide eyes, stupid and plump, merely children. I know I should not, but I am so hungry. They run, but I am in every shadow. I reach into a girl's chest, feasting on a beating heart. I am so ungrateful.

Sixth Mistake
William A. Wellman

"Will you be long in the fields?" my wife asks. Her cold, unsuspecting eyes are devoid of fire. "Until very late," I say, "there's much to harvest."

I leave that stifling house, and the inn is not far. The barkeep knows my face, but my coin keeps him quiet. In my room I heat the wax, dripping patterns across the floor. I fill the hearth with rose petals, then light them. She emerges in smoke, and speaks with ember lips. "We can't keep doing this."

Her lips burn mine as we meet, consuming my soul for one more fervent mistake.

Heartstruck
William A. Wellman

"What is that sound?" She whispers with concern, laying on my chest. She is not the first to press her ear to my skin and wonder.

"My heart requires winding." I say. "I lost mine when I was young, and the alchemist did what he could. Now it is metal; little pieces spinning. If I don't say this every night, they will stop." I show the letters that cover my arm, green like her eyes.

"Can I?" She whispers, tracing the symbols with her finger. I shiver, and nod. My chest tightens as she sings, my life on her lips.

Blood Letter
William A. Wellman

Six times now he has gone out to the fields, yet returned with no harvest. The barkeep's wife tells me that he takes out rooms in the broad daylight, and they smell of incense and roses. I stand over our marriage bed while he snores like a wild pig, and open his book.

He does not know that I, too, have visited the alchemist, that he has taught me to read. He turns in his sleep, and says a name that is not mine. The letters are red like blood on the snow, and I sing softly to unmake him.

One Shadow
William A. Wellman

"Are you ready?" I whisper. The girl with the clockwork heart is behind me; my finest craftsmanship. Every corner is lit with candles, leaving only one shadow in the keep.

Bowstrings creak as archers hold them steady, and she readies her crimson blade. I have shared much of my knowledge with this town; a byproduct of my years of study. I speak the words now—the summoning is the easy part. The shadow comes alive, too many teeth and arms. Arrows pass through it like smoke, but the blood sword cuts deep as my words blaze with light.

No more shadows.

William A. Wellman

William A. Wellman is a queer horror writer and marketing professional who haunts Parc La Fontaine in Montreal. A lifelong lover of meticulously crafted stories, they believe that fiction has a unique power to comfort, terrify, or inspire - and sometimes all at once. When not writing for anthologies or working on novels, they write + produce the horror fiction podcast Hello From The Hallowoods.

You can connect with William on social media at @williamawellman, or learn more about their work at www.williamwellmanwrites.com.

The Sleep Farm
McKenzie Richardson

The air was heavy with slow breathing, countless heads lolling onto chests. As soon as the spindle had pricked the finger every creature dozed off where they stood. Slumbering, unmoving, continually they dreamed.

Not a soul stirred outside the tower, but inside something did.

Sleeping Beauty wasn't sleeping; she was wide awake.

Sharp teeth dripped with crimson as she sunk them into unsuspecting dreams. The ruler of the Land of Sleep watched over her subjects, her magic keeping them alive, until she was ready to harvest them, that is. She'd consume their deepest wishes until they were ready for slaughter.

The Last Lullaby
McKenzie Richardson

The lid of the music box popped open, filling the room with its tinkling song. The air seemed to hold its breath to the slow clicking sound, like raindrops on the rooftop or sand slipping through an hourglass.

Her eyes stared unseeingly into the box's black interior, transfixed by the melody. Many had stared into that abyss, mesmerized into forgetting the world. They ignored hunger, thirst and sleep.

Countless creatures had wasted away to that very song; in time she would join their ranks.

She should have known better than to betray a witch. They always seek the worst revenge.

Eternal Darkness
McKenzie Richardson

Rage reverberates through every fiber of his being. Betrayed by humans once again, he promises this will be the last time.

Power surges through him as he finally gives in to his darker side, tasting its electric current. Anger fueling him he stretches Heavenward, crashing through the canvas of the sky as blue fragments rain down. Clouds burst at his heated touch, evaporating into nothingness.

His shadow looms over the world, larger than trees that have witnessed centuries, larger than mountains that have dared to reach new heights.

In one bite he swallows the sun, plunging the earth into darkness.

To Raise the Dead
McKenzie Richardson

The body hovers over the table, its limp hair swaying. Streams of light encircle it, highlighting the dead skin's graying hue. With a final flash the orbiting lights violently erupt. The corpse slams back heavily onto the table, its eyes jolting open.

Once the chaos settles the newly-resurrected man stares blankly, confused. From the corner a dark shape separates itself from the shadows.

"Good to see you, Magnus," it says.

When his sluggish brain finally recognizes the face, Magnus trembles.

"Why'd you bring me back?"

The necromancer sneers down at him.

"To allow me the pleasure of killing you myself."

Shadows of the Earth
McKenzie Richardson

The shadows crept in quietly, obscuring the moonlight. Having spent their lives in the mines, extracting the earth's treasures, the townspeople had habituated to the dark.

Yet nothing prepared them for what they'd uncovered in the deepest, darkest pits.

Standing at the mouth of the cave she monitored the destruction, amused at their feeble attempts to outrun her shadows. Screams composed a chorus of chaos; no match for the swirling obsidian that raked down throats, ripping them apart from the inside.

When all was still she retreated back to the depths to rest before the next fool interrupted her slumber.

McKenzie Richardson

McKenzie Richardson lives in Milwaukee, WI. A lifelong explorer of imagined worlds on the written page, over the last few years she has been finding homes for her own creations. Most recently, her work has been featured in anthologies by Black Hare Press, Eerie River Publishing, and Iron Faerie Publishing. She has also published a poetry collaboration with Casey Renee Kiser, 433 Lighted Way, and her middle-grade fantasy novel, Heartstrings, is available on Amazon.

http://www.craft-cycle.com
https://www.facebook.com/mckenzielrichardson

The Cellar
Michelle Bryan

She stumbled down the stairs into the darkness below. No one had been here for a long time, yet tonight the cellar was buzzing with expectation. Goosebumps erupted as a hot wind tainted with sulphur drifted up, tickling her nostrils. Evil permeated the air. The portal was near.

Summoning her magic she swallowed her fear, praying she wouldn't mess this up.

No mistakes.

The spell dropped from her ruby lips as the portal shimmered with Hellfire. The demonic figure emerging from the flames sucked greedily at her lifeforce and instilled terror in her heart.

Still, she smiled.

"Welcome home, Dad."

Michelle Bryan

Michelle Bryan is a USA Today Bestselling author. She resides in Nova Scotia, Canada with her three favorite guys; her hubby, son, and fur baby, Garbage.

She is a huge fan of The Walking Dead and Game of Thrones, and never misses an episode. She also believes every day should consist of reading, writing, chocolate, and coffee-not necessarily in that order.

Author of The Crimson Legacy Series, Legacy of Light Series, and The Bixby Series. You can find out more about her books by visiting her website at http://www.michellebryanauthor.com/ or follow her on Goodreads or Facebook.

HAPPPILY EVER AFTER
K.G. Lewis

The knight ran up the steps of the tower, kicking in the door before stepping into the room where the princess was being held prisoner.

"My hero!" the princess beamed, reaching her arms out to her rescuer.

The knight ran over to embrace the beautiful maiden, but his arms passed through her body as if it were made out of smoke.

As the princess disappeared a trapdoor opened beneath the knight; he fell to the bottom of the tower.

The ghost of the princess reappeared next to the knight's lifeless body. "You were too late," she whispered into his ear.

FOR WHOM THE BELL TOLLS
K.G. Lewis

"No!" Theodore cried out, watching his father fall to the ground as blood poured from the wound on his side.

"The bell," his father sputtered, blood bubbling from his lips, "Ring the bell."

Theodore turned and ran through the graveyard, weaving around the tombstones on his way to the church.

"Stop him!" The knight pointed his bloody sword at Theodore.

Once inside Theodore raced across the church, grabbing the rope hanging from the steeple. He pulled on it with all his might. The bell began to toll.

Outside the dead heard the call, then began to rise from their graves.

THE DANCE
K.G. Lewis

The motions of her dance were flawless as she moved from one end of the stage to the other, losing herself in the rhythm of the music.

When the screams began she looked out at the audience for the first time. Blood flowed freely from their eyes and ears as they tried to flee. She couldn't believe what she was seeing. After years of practice she'd finally gotten the steps of the ritual right!

She continued to dance until the music ended and bodies littered the auditorium. Smiling, she walked to the edge of the stage and took a bow.

K.G. Lewis

K.G. Lewis is an American horror author and tabletop game designer (under the name Ken Lewis) residing in Atlanta, GA.

https://www.amazon.com/.../e/B07TWJM7FG/ref=ntt_dp_epwbk_0

Return Policy
Dustin Walker

The parents avoid eye contact with me as I step inside their home.

"We didn't think he'd be like this," the dad whispers.

"Where is he?" I ask. No time for small talk; I have another return to process right after this one.

"Upstairs. First door on your left."

I haul my cage up to the boy's room and step inside. His bloated corpse yanks against the chains holding him to the bed, bits of loose flesh splattering against the walls as he flails.

I sigh and get to work. No one ever thinks long-term when they hire a necromancer.

Bad Drugs
Dustin Walker

The newspapers blamed bad heroin for all the deaths, but I knew city councillors were behind it. Those bastards pumped the streets full of lethal drugs to 'clean up' the homeless population, so I'd give them something else to clean.

The soup kitchen started closing early because of all the so-called overdoses. Not as many mouths to feed, officials said, but that morning a horde waited outside its doors. Bodies shuffled inside, their eyes empty and limbs rigid. They were hungry, but they didn't want food.

As I listened to the screaming I wondered what the newspapers would write tomorrow.

Summer Reading
Dustin Walker

When Tom told me he had read a lot this summer I thought he meant fantasy or sci-fi novels, but the black, fleshy cover of the book he held told me otherwise.

After showing me the grimoire he showed me his new bunny. The thing threw itself against the cage, its bloodied neck twisted at an impossible angle. A circle and jagged symbols had been scrawled onto the plywood floor of its enclosure in black marker.

Tom nudged me and pointed toward the barn at the edge of his family's ranch.

"Summer's not over yet," he said with a grin.

Dustin Walker

Dustin Walker has worked as a dishwasher, a news reporter and a tech marketer. But he's most passionate about writing gritty crime and horror stories. Dustin's fiction has appeared in Yellow Mama, Dark Moon Digest, Pulp Modern and on The NoSleep Podcast. He lives on Vancouver Island, Canada, with his wife and daughter.

The Quill Witch
E. Joan Armstrong

The porcupine familiar licked its master's face, maneuvering quills to avoid tangled hair.

Eyelids flicked open.

3 A.M., the witching hour.

Every incantation cost something, but youthful Yarrow had an invincibility mindset. The initiation shocked her hair white, the subsequent incantation staining her nail beds frosty purple.

Yarrow produced a quill and pricked her finger. Bloody hands held towards the stars she spoke the ritual. Power flowed until she brimmed, a glowing echo of the moon. Blue eyes transitioned to black, glow receding. Her internal power hummed, ready for use, and use it she would.

E. Joan Armstrong

A lifelong fantasy lover, E. Joan Armstrong loves stories that help the reader escape to another reality. Having held a variety of day jobs she now focuses on writing and creative pursuits.

The Basilisk of Barnabas Brimstone
Sandy Butchers

The sign above the circus tent flashed on and off in blue and golden letters: "The Eighth Wonder of the World". Admittance was a penny, two for front row seats.

Barnabas entered the ring to the roaring of the crowd. A deep grin carved his face as he walked to the golden curtain. "Ladies and gentlemen," he started as he took a mirror from his pocket and put on sunglasses, "I give you, the Basilisk of Barnabas Brimstone!"

The curtain fell.

First there was screaming. Then all was quiet in an instant, turned to stone for a penny or two.

The Visitor
Sandy Butchers

Tory ran down the stairs, panting and bathed in sweat. When she opened the door to the pink and purple princess room a scream ripped through the night. She froze and suppressed another scream at the sight of a tiny creature on top of her son, digging its fingers deep into his mouth.

A creak and a crack tore through the silence.

"Tooth Fairy?" Tory whispered.

She watched in horror as the creature flashed a bloodied grin with its mouth full of human teeth.

Children's teeth…her son's teeth.

Blood trickled down the bedsheets. Tory knew enough…she was next.

The Water Horse
Sandy Butchers

Quinn feared he would run out of air before the waves split open above his head. His hands gripped tight around a slippery, slender neck that pulsed with each movement as the surface came closer. The water burst into a bubble of a thousand drops when he could finally breathe again.

Quinn screamed at the sight of the water horse as it beat its fins and scaly tail against the waves, shaking the seaweed from its manes. He could see it smile at him with gnarly teeth, ready to pull him back under. For how long, nobody knew for certain.

The Curious Case of Cassey Coulter
Sandy Butchers

Amidst five burning candles I found her body. They still burned, and the purple tendrils of smoke rising from the flames told me there was more going on than I could dispatch in my report. A failed séance, perhaps? Or a vampire's kiss gone wrong?

The flesh torn from between her neck and shoulder was an awful sight to see. A low growl rumbled to my left, sending me straight into panic as I ran and watched a shadow bend over the corpse. This wasn't a ghost, nor was it a vampire.

I suddenly realized this was Death himself.

Sandy Butchers

Sandy Butchers is an author and an artist known for her elaborate fantasy worlds and creature designs. After living in Scandinavia for a year and traveling throughout the world, she now settled in the countryside, along with a variety of pets and maps on which X marks the spot.

You can find her on Twitter: @SandyButchers
(https://twitter.com/SandyButchers)
Or go to her website for more information:
www.sandybutchers.com

A Mass Grave
Paul Benkendorfer

Abdul stepped onto the field, gazing out at the opposing army standing across from his own: pikes, swords and axes rapped against wooden shields and blue-tinted armour. With thundering roars they charged forwards.

Abdul knelt, placing his palms onto the grass. His eyes became black as ink, veins turning to streams of tar. He muttered enchantments under his breath. Energy surged from his core to his hands, the ground ripping open like an earthquake. Soldiers shrieked, falling into craters and pits, devoured by the Earth. After the last man fell the cavities shut.

The battlefield was now a silent graveyard.

Paul Benkendorfer

Paul Benkendorfer is an AP English teacher from Queen Creek, Arizona. As an educator Paul has worked extensively with at-risk and special needs youth for close to a decade. Paul attended the University of Arizona in Tucson where he received his Bachelor's in Creative Writing. In 2020, Paul earned his Master's in Teaching Writing from The Johns Hopkins University with a focus on how writing can be used to help at-risk youth develop their academic skills and overcome trauma. Paul's work has been featured in several anthologies, journals, and magazines including High Shelf Press, Eerie River Publishing, Black Hare Press, The Write Launch, Allegory Ridge, the Dark Poet's Club as well as many others.

A Technicality
Peter VanGelderen

"Of course!" I unthinkingly said.

The glittery pixies joyfully squealed, their tiny hands wrapping around me. With surprising might they hoisted me upward. Higher we went into the world of birds and fae, and I laughed like never before. I was free for the first time in my life! I didn't even realize how thin the air was getting.

"Okay, that's enough flying for today." One of them giggled.

As their grip loosened I realized they'd said they'd let me fly, but never mentioned bringing me down. My vision darkens; their gleeful, laughing faces are the final things I see.

A Sorcerer's Lament
Peter VanGelderen

Tens of thousands of orcs surround my spire, their battle cries creating a deafening blast of rage as they reach the door to my quarters. My blood magic can only take out two hundred, maybe three, before I collapse from exsanguination. I thought their fear of my power would keep them in line, but the blades and axes taking apart my door tell me I was wrong.

"Kill enslavers! Kill oppressors!" Their guttural voices below.

The door shatters. As they flood the room I dash to the window: dying from gravity is better than facing what they'll do to me.

Just a Little Company
Peter VanGelderen

The bones rise. A viscous, maroon smoke replaces the tendons and ligaments that rotted away long ago. A new soul enters the shambling form, a blank slate ready to learn how to kill.

"Orders, sir?" it asks its maker with a creaky voice.

The wizard pours a steamy, fragrant brew into a small cup and beckons his creation to a comfortable seat. His clothes are torn and ragged from age, and his eyes are teary from loneliness. The necromancer's cane lies near the magically-sealed cave entrance, covered in decades of dust.

"Please, have a seat and chat with me awhile."

Friends in High Places
Peter VanGelderen

Torches light the gravel road leading to my clifftop hovel, where I can hear the furious yells of villagers. It matters not that I cure their sick, safeguard their children from the criminals they refuse to prosecute and empower their downtrodden with knowledge. They still wish to burn me alive because they cannot understand the nature of my talents.

I sigh and call my ancient friend as I begin to pack my effects. "Kill only the worst of them, please."

The portals outside opens, and screams erupt. I slip out the back and begin the search for a new home.

Noble Problems
Peter VanGelderen

The Baronness watches night descend on the village below, quietly sipping her brandy as the peasants rush home to lock their doors and windows for the night.

"Will you be joining the rest of the family this evening?" A servant asks.

"Not tonight, I'm quite tired. Perhaps tomorrow."

He bows. "Very good, ma'am."

Screams rise from the town. There are always some who don't make it home in time. Abominable growls, and the sounds of tearing flesh, begin.

The Baroness sighs. "Make sure the water buckets are filled. I won't have Uncle dripping blood on the rugs again."

Peter VanGelderen

I am a Michigan based author attempting to break into the world of fantasy and horror writing. I am currently featured in the Reign of Queens anthology from Dragon Soul Press with my short story, "Wolves," and will be featured in their upcoming September anthology, Lethal Impact, with my story titled "Below." I also currently have an unpublished novel, as well as several other projects that I'm working on. I am doing my best to expand and build a name for myself in the world of fiction.

Link: https://www.facebook.com/PeterVanGelderenBooks/

The Violinist
B.B. Blazkowicz

Rural towns always draw the best crowds. I stand in the town square, pull my hair back and then begin playing my violin. Like rats to the pied piper scores of them gather to hear. My dynamic melodies adjust to the second with their shifting emotions. Curiosity, surprise and wonder.

Then the passages turn melancholy; with that comes despair. I see their sadness. I hear them weep, but they are frozen stiff with fear. My violin rings out with dissonance and atonality, the breeze becoming a gust. Finally, after I resolve the final chord, they all fall, never to rise.

The Northern Cold
B.B. Blazkowicz

I sit at the longhouse's dying hearth just as my ancestors did before me, only I now do so alone. I can travel no further across this land of frozen trees and blinding, white wind. I have failed them all.

They were taken by the disembodied spirits who walk among the ice, now wearing the frozen, hollow-eyed faces of my former kin. I watch them grow closer as the flame dims and feel their grip on my back tighten. I lack the strength and the will to resist as they begin pulling me from the smoldering embers into oblivion's embrace.

B.B. Blazkowicz

B.B. Blazkowicz is a horror fiction writer currently tied to a chair in an Antarctic research facility. A bearded man who smells of Scotch says one of us is assimilated. If you are reading this please send me transportation to your densest population centers.

He Awakens
Adrian J. Johnson

Damien wakes up with a sharp, aching pain in the back of his head, only to find himself in a small, yet unfamiliar room.

There are four other men in the room with him, and each of them is positioned on a point of the chalk outline of a pentagram. They're sprawled on the plank floor, blood seeping out of the back of their skulls.

Each man grips a handgun which once contained a single bullet. Damien notices the handgun in his hand, and uses his free hand to feel the bullet wound he inflicted himself.

He has been chosen.

Adrian J. Johnson

Adrian J. Johnson is an American author of dark fiction. Most of his work has appeared in numerous anthologies, available in print, eBook, and audio formats. He is also the owner of Red Masque Media, a freelance graphic design company specializing in multimedia designs for dark-themed genres. He lives in Ohio with his family.

You can follow Adrian J. Johnson and Red Masque Media on Facebook, Twitter, and Instagram, or contact them via email at realadrianjamesjohnson@gmail.com and redmasquemedia@gmail.com.

Teach Them Terror
Constantine E. Kiousis

Laying perched on the edge of a cliff she glared at the village below, observing the ants as they ambled around while smiling, laughing and bragging. Her children, in full display near the village square, dripped blood from their hanged corpses as they dangled above the crimson-stained ground. She had been too trusting, too merciful.

She should have never left her offspring alone.

Wings spreading, she leaped from the precipice, descending upon the settlement. She would teach them terror. Eyes glinting, her jaws parted, bright fire blasting forth from her throat to engulf everything.

Their screams filled the cold night.

Prisoner
Constantine E. Kiousis

He pressed himself against the inner, crystalline wall of the emerald as he pounded at it, screaming to be let out. Outside, everything looked gargantuan. How had this happened? He was sure he'd chanted the words right, the ones scribbled on the papyrus he'd discovered inside the ornate box.

A large figure approached the fallen, precious stone, picking it up and bringing it close to its face. The prisoner's eyes widened as he saw his own visage staring back at him, grinning.

"Gratitude for the vessel," said the stranger wearing his body. "It's been too long since I've been out."

Fireflies
Constantine E. Kiousis

The girl fell down on her knees, face smudged by soot as she gawked at the small house in front of her, flames consuming it as if nothing but kindling. The wood crackled, sparks flying against the dark sky like fireflies.

How could she have been so careless? Her father had warned her not to read from the tome, had warned her of the danger, but the pull had been too strong. The arcane blood coursing through her veins constantly called to her.

Her parents were still screaming when the roof collapsed, and then there was only the hissing fire.

The Price
Constantine E. Kiousis

The old man shielded his eyes as cold air blew past him, his hair and robes ruffling as the fabric of reality fractured in front of him like transparent glass. Pallid light seeped through the cracks. He swallowed hard as the fissures spread, pieces of existence falling and shattering on the stone floor. It revealed an amorphous mass, black, twisting and coiling against the sickly glow.

He glanced down, towards the disemboweled body of the child lying in the crimson ritual circle. His son's blurry eyes stared at him, almost accusatory, face twisted in agony.

A necessary price to pay.

Until Dawn
Constantine E. Kiousis

The crone leaned towards the boy, beady eyes boring into him.

"Second thoughts?" she crooned.

He shook his head, scowling through swollen eyes.

"Vengeful little thing," she cackled, face darkening. "Very well. You'll have until dawn," she warned, "and then I'll come collect, understood?"

He nodded.

The hag grinned, midnight air stirring as she began the chant, eldritch, forbidden words leaving her chapped lips as the boy's body twisted, flesh tearing, bones breaking and rearranging as his cries turned to guttural growls.

A beast towered where a child once stood. Howling, it went on the prowl.

It had their scent.

WHISPERS
Constantine E. Kiousis

Roland leaned over his younger brother's body, face pale as he stared at the smoke billowing from the crater of charred flesh and bone on the child's chest. Little Arlie's clouded eyes gazed lifelessly at the gray sky above.

The boy gawked at the intricate stick laying on the ground beside his feet, a thing made of twisting twigs with a tiny, ebony stone at the top. He'd found it in their father's attic, heard it whispering through a pile of baubles, calling his name. Next thing he knew, he was here.

The wand lay silent now; so did Arlie.

Constantine E. Kiousis

Constantine E. Kiousis spends most of his time wandering through the worlds he has created, exploring every nook and cranny and constantly discovering new places and stories that need to be told. He is in the company of his fictional characters more often than he likes to admit, sharing in their ordeals and times of joy, and has had some very interesting conversations, as well as legendary arguments, with many of them.

He currently resides in Athens, Greece, plotting ways to unleash the terrifying stories hiding in his mind upon the rest of the world, one word at a time.

You can keep up with his work by visiting his author page: https://www.facebook.com/KiousisStoryteller

Throwing the Bones
Mary Rajotte

Midnight descends on the Bayou. Crickets chatter. Bats flutter. Voices eons old linger in ghostly tendrils of swaying Spanish moss above Adelle's head, enticing her to tempt fate.

The storm water recedes, unearthing a bone in the muck - treasure only Adele dares to touch.

She snatches it, adds it to buttons and shells. Shakes them together with a hollow clack, tossing them into the simmering brew.

When the drink is ready, and the bone leeched of all power, Adele slurps it down without restraint. Sated, her new reflection appears in the brackish water. Darkness within her, now nourished, thrives.

Inscribed
Mary Rajotte

With centuries of dust carefully brushed from the elaborate coffin, the Pharaoh's face is revealed.

John is compelled to turn away, but something glimmers in the obsidian, painted eyes.

He pauses, fingers outstretched, then sweeps away grit from the lid's ancient inscriptions.

Motes dance in the shafts of light like the whispers of ancient prayers. Sun shines on gold lettering, warming and bringing the ancient words back to life.

Leaning over, John is compelled to speak. The incantation, now whispered, invokes the ancient hex. It works anew, turning his skin to weathered parchment.

And, inside the coffin, the Pharaoh stirs.

Forewarned

Mary Rajotte

On the great oak outside her isolated cabin Isobel carves a sigil for protection; afterwards she barricades the doors and lights a fire for comfort.

Something strikes the window.

Hoping the darkness will swallow her fears she peers out. The faint imprint of feathers obscures the window. Below a bird twitches, then falls still.

In the dead of night comes another strike. Looking out this time Isobel finds a ghostly imprint.

There is no feathery down, no wings splayed, no tail feathers in stark relief.

Instead, the imprint is the face of a haggard crone, come to exact her vengeance.

Beneath the Skin
Mary Rajotte

Sonic soundscapes envelop the interior of the darkened nightclub. The drum track is Evie's heartbeat, the strobe lights her pulse. The tang of sweat in the air brings a tingle to her skin, awakening the power she harbors within.

But even here she is hunted, the shadows not deep enough to keep her hidden.

When the bass drops she dashes for the dance floor. Overhead black light invokes the true power she conceals. Marks, hidden under normal light, burn to life. Sigils, indelible in their luminescence, glow brightly, protection no one can thwart. Reenergized, Evie's powers pulse, revive, and thrive.

Mary Rajotte

Canadian author Mary Rajotte has a penchant for penning nightmarish tales of folk horror and paranormal suspense. Her work has been published in Shroud Magazine, The Library of Horror Press, the Great Lakes Horror Company, Magnificent Cowlick Media, Fabled Collective and Burial Day Books. Sometimes camera-elusive but always coffee-fueled, you can find Mary at her website http://www.maryrajotte.com or support her Patreon for exclusive fiction at patreon.com/maryrajotte

Dumped
Belinda Brady

"You're too clingy, moody and vindictive. I'm done!" Rick screams, slamming the front door.

Aghast, I stare after him. Those admirable traits are just the tip of my wicked, tainted iceberg - I'm much darker than that.

Time to show him the real me.

The night is still as I climb through his bedroom window. He wakes when I straddle him, my strength pinning him down.

"You forgot vengeful," I snarl.

I inhale deeply, his fading essence filling my lungs, his body crumbling to dust beneath me.

Since he didn't appreciate my dead soul, he could at least feed it.

Belinda Brady

A bookworm since childhood, Belinda is passionate about stories and after years of procrastinating, has finally turned her hand to writing them, with a preference for supernatural/thriller themes; both often competing for her attention. She has had several stories published in a variety of publications, both online and in anthologies. Belinda lives in Australia with her family and has been known to enjoy the company of cats over people.

Evocation
Damien Allmark

The candles flickered; Celeste was not alone in her own head. She smirked in spite of herself. Flashes of yellow, slitted eyes, horns and a tail filled her consciousness.

A hot wind blew through the basement. The flames danced, then expired. Power over the entity slid from her grasp, slippery, thrashing, like a freshly caught fish. Celeste's smile vanished. Her heart thundered and ice seized her spine. She wrestled in vain to regain control.

Fangs, wet with spittle, bared into a monstrous grin.

"FREEDOM."

Cerebral tentacles constricted her vision, and Celeste's life ended to the sound of a baritone laugh.

Failure

Damien Allmark

The elven girl scrambled backwards on the loose shale beach. "No, please!"

"You have failed me, Kintella. I do not tolerate failure."

Selmana extended her arm, palm up, and clenched her fist.

Kintella's plea halted and she reached for her throat. Panic filled her eyes as she fought for breath. "Please," she croaked.

Selmana opened her hand.

Kintella flopped to the ground and gasped cold, refreshing air into her lungs. "Thank you."

Selmana cocked her head to one side and her icy, grey eyes twinkled. "For what?" Her hand closed again, and she squeezed the life from her sister's body.

City Defender
Damien Allmark

Countless white sails filled the cove, and cannon fire rained down on the port of Adderly Bay.

"I can help," begged Darian. "Please." He held up his manacles, the sigils glowing an arcane green.

Osvaldo muttered incantations, and Darian's restraints fell away.

Darian raised both hands, then roiling, black clouds filled the sky. Bolt after bolt of lightning pounded the ships until the entire armada was ablaze.

Osvaldo trained his crossbow on Darian, and held out the manacles.

Darian smirked.

Osvaldo loosed the bolt, but it found no target.

Cackling filled the air, and lightning started to strike the city.

Patronage Revoked
Damien Allmark

"I beseech you, Lord, permit me to keep the power you bestow." Daveth stretched his hand in front of him, and flames ignited at each fingertip. Relief flooded through him. "Thank you, Master. I will repay your faith." He closed his fist, which should extinguish the blaze.

The fire quivered, but remained.

Burgeoning warmth spread from the conjuration like never before. He shook his hand, but the heat spread up his wrist. Flames licked at his arms and gnawed the cuff of his robe. Daveth's screams morphed from fear to agony, and he clawed at his arm as he crumpled.

Highway Robbery
Damien Allmark

"Gimme the money, girl," the thug growled.

Daphne's voice was melodious. "No, thank you."

"And what's a little bitch like you gonna do about it?"

Daphne's eyes rolled back until they were flawless white. Words in a language lost to the earth reverberated from her, fanged jaws open in an abyssal snarl.

The thug watched with terror-filled eyes as his hand flipped the dagger, unbidden, and his fist closed around the hilt. The sun glinted on the tip of the blade as his trembling fist aligned it to his eye and drove it deep into his skull.

Daphne giggled. "That."

Damien Allmark

Damien is a fledgling author who has previously been published in Dark Dossier magazine, Sword & Sorcery magazine and Ariel Chart. When not wrestling with the keyboard you'll find him behind the wheel of a bus or at home in Bristol, England with his newborn son. For more information and upcoming projects check him out at damien-allmark.co.uk

Shipwrecked
Darlene Holt

Harsh sunlight pierces my eyes. A mass of corpses. Remnants of entrails among debris. Then I hear it. Crooning—a lullaby—calling me.

Passing cragged cliffs I discover mist-shrouded silhouettes perched on ashen rocks beyond the swelling surf. Glistening, golden hair. Shimmering tails.

Intoxicated by their voices, I trek on.

But soon day ruptures into night. Their gleaming skin turns sallow; bones protrude through flaking scales. Sunken, bare-breasted chests expose blackened, beating hearts.

Yet I trudge into the water, surrender to the cold, elongated fingers clutching my throat. Deafened by the sirens' song.

Dance of the Dryad
Darlene Holt

"Why are nymphs only female?" he asks, raising the goblet to his lips. He caresses her as they lay, unclothed, in the hollowed-out oak. "I've seen no males in these woods, dryad or otherwise."

She sensually slides her legs away, her spring-green skin blending perfectly with the foliage-strewn floor. Beautifully embellished vines wrap around her curves. "Men serve only a single purpose," she says. Pressing a palm to her stomach she senses the seedling of an unborn daughter pulsating in her womb. The dryad smiles. "More mead, my love?"

His goblet falls from hand, eyes rolling back into his head.

Deadly Legends
Darlene Holt

Galloping deep in the Black Forest its shadowy body is set aglow, moonlight breaking through evergreens. I mustn't lose it.

The beast halts between trees, tossing its head wildly. Its sable mane becomes tousled, a spiraled, obsidian horn jutting from its forehead. I step closer, one hand outstretched, the other wielding my switchblade. Haunting, crimson eyes pierce into me. My heart races.

Drinking the blood of a dark beast is said to give immortality.

Bucking violently as I approach, it rages and lowers its head—impales me with the great, black horn—and drinks the blood spilling from my innards.

Beneath the Surface
Darlene Holt

"If she sinks, she's pure!" the townspeople spew, tightening my knots. "But if she floats she's a witch, and she'll burn!"

I'm lifted over a hoard of torches, a cacophony of sloshing boots and clanging pitchforks permeating the air.

"Witch!" they chant. "Demon! Devil!" Murky water soaks their knees. They topple my chair over, and I break the lake's eerily placid surface.

I sink.

But soon I transform, bursting from my bindings—from my human body—tentacles slapping the lake's surface into raging waves. I thrash the crowd with them, torches flying, laughing as villagers fall with heavy, lifeless thumps.

Darlene Holt

Darlene Holt is a writer, editor, and educator. Her most recent fiction appears in Sirens Call Publications, Black Hare Press' Dark Moments, and Horror Tree's Trembling with Fear. She especially enjoys writing drabbles with several appearing in Black Hare Press' forthcoming drabble anthologies. She has an MA in English and Creative Writing and currently resides in San Diego, California, where she enjoys reading horror stories and spending time with her husband and cats.

Rise and Fall
Lauraine S. Blake

"Rise, Daemon. Come up and take flight." The words ripple over his skin. Pale skin. Sickly skin. Painted with dark lines – dark magic.

I hate him.

The air becomes smoke: suspended, unbreathable, ebony particulates. I hate that too, the sulfurous stench of it.

"Rise." A hum grows on his tongue. Resonating, stroking tenderly down my spine. It sets loose thirst; my wildest desires and cruelest fantasies.

I rise.

Black-clawed and obsidian-winged, I arch towards him. I want him. Yet, as I reach for him – taloned hand outstretched – he recoils, disgusted.

I hate him.

It takes only one lunge.

He falls.

Lauraine S Blake

Lauraine S Blake, author of 'The Wilder Light,' is an emerging British writer. She loves to leave the real world and delve into the realms of fantasy — mostly dark fantasy and occasionally horror. In love with books from a young age, she decided to stare down dyslexia and just be a writer anyway. In her other life, she's an astrophysicist and tutor who delights in maths and science. Her up and coming work can be found in Eerie River's 'Bone and Iron' anthology, Black Hare Press's '666' and 'Bones' anthologies as well as Dominion Press's 'Dark Towers,' 'Dark Magic' and 'Dark Servants' anthologies. To find out more about her work, please visit www.thewilderlight.com

The Destroyer
Charlotte Langtree

They watched from afar, enamoured by her beauty. Golden hair fell in ringlets to frame an angelic face. She served a cruel master, a man so vile he'd sewn her mouth shut to prevent her complaints.

The young men could bear it no longer. Swords drawn, they restrained the furious nobleman and cut the stitches along her lips.

"No!" the nobleman screamed.

As the last stitch came loose, the woman's face distorted. Her mouth elongated, revealing a black void that seeped into the air. The demon swallowed each man whole.

She was the Destroyer of Worlds, and she was free.

The Garden of Lost Souls
Charlotte Langtree

He should have known better than to offer flowers to a fey princess. She almost loved him, but she could never forget the dichotomy of his soul. He was a romantic man, a poet, and an executioner with blood on his hands.

They were her favourite, those souls poisoned by their dark deeds. His tainted soul danced in her hand as she planted it in the rich soil. All flourished in her garden, from lowly beggars to valiant knights, weeping and wailing among the roses and the sweet-scented jasmine.

It was a garden fit for the queen she would become.

The Hunt
Charlotte Langtree

Snowy feathers drifted through a crisp sky as the owl hunted her prey, moonlight glinting off her outstretched claws. She screeched once, the sound echoing through the eerie night as she spotted her prey, then swooped down.

At the last moment the air shimmered wildly, and her shape blurred and changed. Human now, she landed atop the escaping warlock, sending him tumbling to the soft ground. Her attack was swift; the warlock's blood painted the snowy canvas a deep crimson. Her owl eyes blinked slowly as she licked the blood from one long finger.

It had been a good hunt.

A Taste of Murder
Charlotte Langtree

The body pulsed with tainted magic. Jennica studied him, ignoring the clamour of the tavern's crowd.

One of them was a killer.

With a touch, she saw his final moments. The taste of his death caused a rush of power that made the room spin. Searching the crowd, she recognized a pale face.

The woman ran, but Jennica was ready. A flick of her hand froze the woman to the spot.

"Take her."

She dismissed the others, then knelt to kiss the dead man's lips. Latching onto his power, she sucked deeply; there was no point in wasting a death.

Charlotte Langtree

Charlotte Langtree is a poet, aspiring novelist, and writer of short fiction. She's been creating stories for almost as long as she has been alive, and has a profound respect for the magic of the written word. She has been published in several magazines and anthologies. In December 2020, she was named 'Author of the Month' by Paper Djinn Press. You can find her online at www.charlottelangtree.wordpress.com, and on Facebook at www.facebook.com/CharlotteLangtreeAuthor.

The Reaper
Diana Allgair

The Reaper observed her palms. Other than the shaking they were still the same small, ink-stained hands prior to her christening. Darkness encircled her wrists and melted into the lines etched across her palms. Deep swirls traced up her fingers and covered her last sense of familiarity in a blanket of black. A cape materialized atop her shoulders and spread to her feet. The weight of the material nearly overwhelmed her, but the newest claimer of souls bore the burden in silence. She held a cane-sized scythe with trembling hands and stared into the tired eyes of her first victim.

The Importance of Silence
Diana Allgair

Massive, crimson scales lined the ancient beast–save its pale underbelly. Steam flowed through its crater-sized nostrils with each exhale, spreading like a dense fog across the cobblestone below. Gold piled behind the dragon in organized pillars. Women raced to add to the beast's collection and remained silent as the creature slept, until a clumsy girl dropped a single coin. It clattered to the floor, and the metallic ring echoed throughout the massive cavern. The dragon's eyelid flickered open to reveal a lime-green sclarea and a blackened rhombus iris. The creature's gaze danced to the girl, then she was no more.

It Lurks Beneath
Diana Allgair

The lake's surface sliced in two as the upper half of a tailed creature surfaced for air. Her hair gathered in clumps akin to seaweed; her chest remained bare to lure feeble-minded men to their doom. One approached, shouting obscenities in a drunken fury. The mermaid's eyes darkened to slits that remained focused on the boat despite the murky water. She slipped underneath the midnight sheet and became nothing more than a darkened, undetectable shape. With a swift flick of her tail the boat toppled over. Bubbles consumed a terrified scream, and in time the lake was still once more.

Diana Allgair

Diana Allgair is an emerging writer and holds a Bachelor of Fine Arts in Motion Picture Arts. She is pursuing a Master of Fine Arts in Creative Writing. Diana currently resides in Florida with her family and her dog, Nami.

Bones, Then Horns, Then Udders
B. J. Thrower

For the 'crime' of throwing rocks at him, a passing warlock changed Alice the Shrew's dairy herd into skeletons, with sharp horns and rotten udders! Afterwards, the buckets were filled with shiny-pink, blood-tinged milk.

Alice was a mean, fat drab. Seated on a stool in the milch shed she *dripped* in the heat, wishing she could take off her skin and sit in her bones.

Mimi, Alice's fat drab of a daughter, whined. "Whadda we d*o*, Ma?"

"Fetch saffron, ninny. Use a pestle, mix it with turmeric. It'll turn this mess yellow, then we can sell it as salty milk."

Bones, Then Teeth, Then Wings
B. J. Thrower

The castle ruins seemed inviting for shelter, until Ragnar the Fool struck a time-weakened hex-wall with his sword to salute the gods.

Fáfnir the Dragon burst forth from its crumbling crypt, a massive, flightless skeleton flapping bony wings. We fled, listening to the music of Ragnar's screams.

I'm the sole survivor. I roll over a cliff, falling twenty feet to a rocky ledge—perhaps it won't eat a woman.

Now Fáfnir's jagged teeth splatter blood down on me. Desperate, I launch into the air toward the sea one hundred feet below. Can Fáfnir fly with gaps in its wings?

Yes.

B. J. Thrower

B. J. Thrower is experiencing a publishing resurgence, selling twelve new stories in two years. Her latest, co-authored with Karen Thrower, is to Sliced-Up Press for Bodies Full of Burning: An Anthology of Menopause-Related Horror, with a s&s novelette upcoming in Weirdbook #49. Recent publications included short stories in Todd Sullivan Presents: The Vampire Connoisseur, and at The Were-Traveler, Issue #22, Women Destroy Retro Sci-Fi. She's previously published in Asimov's, in the 2019 anthology Guilty Pleasures and Other Dark Delights by thingsinthewell.com (a double-drabble), and many others. A SFWA member, she's the 2021 VP of OSFW (Oklahoma Science Fiction Writers). Find her on Facebook, or her website: http://bjthrower.osfw.online. She lives in a bedroom community of Tulsa, OK, with her husband, the mysterious "R."

White Cat
Thomas Sturgeon Jr

The spell had left the young man transformed into a white feline, and in order to break the curse he had to kill the witch who placed it upon him.

The silence in the cathedral made him shiver with anticipation as he awaited a righteous moment to change back to what he previously was throughout the years. Crows flew, cackling as the cat waited for his opportunity to strike when the witch wasn't expecting him.

He jumped straight into her face, clawing out her eyeballs as she screamed hollowly, then the witch laughed as she absorbed his soul forever.

Thomas Sturgeon Jr

Thomas Sturgeon Jr is an 35 year old author living in Chatsworth Georgia. He is the author of "Red Carnival" on Amazon. He has been featured in 32 anthologies since 2018. You can find him on Facebook. He has a cat named Tigger whom he loves dearly. He loves his family and friends. He loves horror and sci-fi.

The Second Wave
Nerisha Kemraj

For the second time in centuries Sirens and Mermaids rose from the salty sea, Fairies gathering from all the lands. Angels flew down from the Heavens, and Officials from the fires of Hell gathered.

It was time.

"I'm sure you know why we're here...They're destroying our homes, and all the elements with it. We can no longer remain silent," said the leader of the Angels.

"Yes. We know what must be done."

A demon official pulled out a burning scroll.

'When Humans are no longer worthy.'

Then they held hands, joining each element to follow through with human extinction.

Discovered
Nerisha Kemraj

Saggio watched his brothers and sisters fall to the floor - a losing battle.

The trolls had discovered their home; they had to summon Chiron before they were all dead.

He signaled to the others, and using the last of their strength the centaurs stomped their hooves, creating a crack through the forest.

Some of the trolls fell to their deaths, and others used logs as bridges while the centaurs summoned Chiron with their magical pendulums.

But the trolls reached them sooner than anticipated, and Centaur blood covered the ground. A dying Saggio saw his god arrive, far too late.

Sacrifice
Nerisha Kemraj

A black puff of smoke rose through the sky.

Hilda found them, according to plan. Now the spell would work.

The four witches held hands around their prisoner.

"Stop! This is not the way. We do not need to sacrifice a sorcerer to be heard!"

"No, Hilda, this is the only way. The Council does not see them as a threat. It's the only way to save our kind." Mayora signaled for the others to grab Hilda's hands, completing the pentagram as they chanted the magic words.

Hilda watched in horror as they captured his soul in the glass vial.

Nerisha Kemraj

Nerisha Kemraj resides in Durban, South Africa with her husband and two mischievous daughters. While poetry has been a love since high school, she began writing short stories in late 2016.

A lover of dark fiction, she has over 180 short stories and poems published in various publications, both print and online. She has also received an Honourable Mention Award for her tanka in the Fujisan Taisho 2019 Tanka Contest.

Nerisha holds a Bachelor's degree in Communication Science, and a Post Graduate Certificate in Education from University of South Africa.

Find her here: https://linktr.ee/NerishaKemraj

BLOOD-RED LIPS
Sheldon Woodbury

The wrinkled, old wizard dragged the young maiden to his underground lair beneath the haunted forest. He'd found her wandering alone in a tattered robe, one splattered with arcane symbols. Her tangled hair was as dark as night, unleashing his repressed, forbidden desires.

Torches burned as he cast a devious spell and began his unwanted seduction. A mischievous smile crept to her blood-red lips, and she whispered one of her witch's quips. Flames erupted around her eternally-young body as she shivered with a morbid joy. Nothing gave her more giggling pleasure than using her vengeful magic on dirty old men.

SHELDON WOODBURY

Sheldon Woodbury is an award winning writer (screenplays, plays, books, short stories, and poems). His book "Cool Million" is considered the essential guide to writing high concept movies. His short stories and poems have appeared in many horror anthologies and magazines. His novel "The World on Fire" was published September, 2014 by JWK Fiction. His poem, The Midnight Circus, was selected by Ellen Datlow as an honorable mention for Best Horror 2017.

Maven's Arrow
A.S. MacKenzie

Tumbling down the embankment he cut himself on the exposed bone fragments, discarded armor and fractured skulls. He skidded to a halt at the bottom, skin on fire from the lacerations. Blood mixed with his sweat, giving each incision their own constant source of pain. Attempting to not think about the potential for infections he most surely now had, he looked back up to see the Maven at the edge. "Why!?" he yelled. The Maven said nothing, but signaled to her undead archers. Getting to his feet he yelled only half of the incantation before an arrow found his throat.

Forever Mine
A.S. MacKenzie

She felt the weight of the painting's stare. Knowing she wasn't his first queen she had hoped to be the last. His first wife, a woman the servants whispered about in fear, made that possibility difficult as she stared down from the canvas. Deciding to end this dead woman's grip on the psyche of this keep, she reached up with a candle and made to light the canvas to finally have peace.

"Your sorcery could not save your life, and cannot save you now," she said wryly. The flame blew out with a breath and a chuckle, neither her own.

Desperate
A.S. MacKenzie

Hands reached out from every dark corner of the room where the flickering light of his candle couldn't reach, fingers desperately groping for contact with any living thing. Lifting the candle from its holder he spoke the scroll's strange words, the other four candles around him lighting verdant flames of their own. When five candles burned bright he could see the hands pulling back into the mire of oblivion. Dozens of pairs of eyes reflected off of the five candles, hungry in their ochre glow, each waiting for the man to drift to sleep and the candles to burn low.

A.S. MacKenzie

A.S. MacKenzie is an Atlanta based author who loves all things thriller, sci-fi, horror, comics, and fantasy. His work includes shorts, novellas, a novel, and several ongoing serial stories through his monthly newsletter. You can find him most days on Twitter (@a_s_mackenzie) going on and on about comics, movies, music, books, and so much more. Also, he is on Instagram (@a.s.mackenzie) where he shows off his love of cooking, travel, and other bits of randomness. He lives with his wife and two weirdo dogs. (he/him) Head to www.asmackenzie.com for some free short stories and how to sign up for the newsletter to read the exclusive serial stories. Unwelcome Space and other Stories is available now through Demain Publishing; It Calls from the Forest v2 is available now through Eerie River Publishing; Three short form eBooks for free download through Prolific Works.

The Arcane Amateur
Brandan Hingley - Lovatt

Elijah Gray ignored the warnings; he was ready, he believed.

He opened the grimoire and read the passage at least a dozen times. Finally, convinced he could do it, he took his blade and nicked the point of his index finger.

"Lupis incarte sana," he murmured.

The wound began to heal, then it stopped. Next it began to widen and spread, new tears of flesh beginning to appear all over his body.

Elijah Gray didn't have the opportunity to scream, instead the tendons and muscles beneath his skin became exposed to air and light for the first, and last, time.

Resurrection Men
Brandan Hingley - Lovatt

Grave robbing is a grim profession, but for the likes of Harris and Maken it was a profitable one. They dug into the ground beneath an old gravestone, of which belonged to that of an alchemist who had been dead for close to three centuries.

The rotten coffin lid gave way easily. Both men were perplexed by the state of the corpse. What should have been bones was instead a gaunt, old man, his skeletal hands clutching a book with gold embroidery. Maken made to grab the book, but was stopped when one of the wizened hands grabbed his wrist.

Tears for the Dead
Brandan Hingley - Lovatt

The witches burned, the crowd watching in silence.

All but one of the condemned screamed. The flames roared at her feet, and soon the flesh on her legs began to bubble and sear. She winced, but held her lips tightly together. Her gaze met all the watchers' eyes as the raging fire consumed more of her body. She spoke something that none of them could hear over the hissing blaze and screams of other condemned dark arts practitioners.

Only when the people looked to one another, and saw tears of blood running down their cheeks, did they break their silence.

Never Look at Its Face
Terrence McKinnies

"Never look at its face!" Mom told me when I mentioned the strange figure that had been following us. She locked the door with all the locks Dad installed yesterday.

"It was just a person."

"It's not a person, it's a monster," Mom said.

"Now go to bed!"

"Okay," I mumbled as I walked to my bedroom.

A sensation struck my heart before I pushed the door open.

On the bed was a figure, its head turned.

He was me, but older.

"Hello, changeling," he coughed, "I guess our parents are happy with what they got: a healthy, eternal child."

Terrence McKinnies

Terrence McKinnies is an educator who is thankful for the boundless joy and invigoration his students and wife bring into his life and writing hobby.

If you rather hear his voice, you can catch him as a guest speaker with the girls of the "Paranoia Percentage" podcast on their recent Mothman episode.

A Promise Kept
Peter Andrew Smith

Karl slit the throat of the man and watched the altar grow red.

"Give me another life," the bloody stone whispered. "I am so hungry."

"I will," Karl pledged, "if you give me magic to force others to obey my will."

"Touch, and receive."

Karl reached out his hands and felt the magic flowing into him. He lifted his right hand, instantly knowing he possessed the power to rule the world. His left hand suddenly grabbed the knife, pulling it across his throat, and as Karl lay dying on the stone the laughter of the blood altar echoed around him.

Daddy's Little Girl
Peter Andrew Smith

Kate looked up from her printing. "Mommy, how do you spell suicide?"

"S-u-i-c-i-d-e." Julie drank from her mug. "Why do you want to know how to spell that word?"

"I want to make sure I get it right in the note you leave."

"What note?" Julie stared at the residue in the bottom of her drink. The room started to spin and she collapsed on the floor. "How could you?"

"I'm not the one who slept with an incubus." Kate tucked the note into Julie's hand and started to chalk a pentagram. "Daddy said I could come live with him."

Peter Andrew Smith

Peter Andrew Smith lives and writes fiction and non fiction in a small town on the East Coast of Canada. He shares his life with his patient wife and daughter and shares a house with a small dog who tolerates no foolishness or dark magic. Peter's recent and older publications can be found listed on his website at http://www.peterandrewsmith.com

Longevity
Chris Lilienthal

The dying wizard confided in his servant the secret to his longevity. Lucius couldn't hear what he said, so he leaned in closer and muttered, "What magic is this, sire?"

But it was too late. The wizard passed, and his body vanished.

On his way back to the cottage Lucius observed a wolf stalking him from behind a large rock. "Show yourself!" he demanded.

The grey wolf strolled out and licked his chops.

Lucius reached for the talisman, but it was gone. It had vanished with everything else the wizard owned.

"Betrayal," the wolf said, echoing the wizard's dying secret.

The Dead Room
Chris Lilienthal

Arthur and Clarisse were hit with a cool rush of air in the room where the family kept their dead.

Long-departed grandparents and relatives lined the walls, sitting in straight-back chairs with their arms suspended in midair. The children could feel the magic coursing through the floorboards and the walls -- the room vibrated with the energy of the dead.

Arthur smiled. "See, nothing scary about it at all."

"We should go, right now," Clarisse said.

Arthur strolled past a dead grandfather. He felt the tight grip around his wrist, just as Clarisse shrieked and the dim, yellow light went out.

Chris Lilienthal

Chris Lilienthal is a dark fiction writer whose work has been published in anthologies from Eerie River Publishing and featured on The Other Stories podcast. He lives with his wife, two sons, and two dogs. Follow him on Twitter @ChrisLilienthal.

The Pain of Vengeance
K.B. Elijah

Bloodless eyes stare up at me, the pale, sackcloth flesh staining beneath my dirty fingers as her limbs sag in my arms.

Miss Rosa's mouth is stretched into a cruel, mocking smile that may be lifeless, but still sears my soul in piercing torment.

"Damn you," I whisper. "Damn you to Hell for what you took from me!"

I take up a glistening needle and slam it down into the doll's heart, gasping as something buffets my own chest. Too late, I notice the band of auburn hair wrapped around the effigy's wrist, the same sunset colors as my own.

Was it Worth it?
K.B. Elijah

"How do I die?" I ask solemnly.

I see my answer materialize, a slip of paper nesting in a writhing mound of maggots that appear on the table. I pinch it between two fingers, brushing off the maggots that cling to me as I pull my hand back.

But they are stuck fast, as if with the fiercest of magnets, their unnaturally hard bodies resisting my attempts to swat them. I shriek as my flesh blisters beneath their touch as they swarm up my arm, consuming both skin and bones.

The paper falls from my fingers. *Eaten alive*, it reads.

Thrice to Thine and Thrice to Mine
K.B. Elijah

"Tell me again," Getra wailed, "why I can't come along?"

"Stop sulking," Villy snapped, dipping the ladle into the vile broth of their cauldron and slurping noisily.

"It's quite clear, Getra," Rawek said, bursting a pus-filled pimple on her bulbous nose. "Macbeth meets three witches on the 'blasted heath'."

"It has to be three," Kuve added, coughing up brown phlegm. "It's the magic number."

She flinched as Villy slumped to the ground beside them, froth foaming in her beard and her eyes wide. Lifeless.

"How convenient," Getra hissed, hiding her sparking fingers behind her back. "Guess I'm coming after all."

K.B. Elijah

K.B. Elijah is a fantasy author living in Brisbane, Australia with her husband and three cockatiels. A lawyer by day, and a writer by...also day, because she needs her solid nine hours of sleep per night (not that the cockatiels let her sleep past 6am).

K.B. writes for various international anthologies, and her work features in dozens of collections about the mysterious, the magical and the macabre. Her own books of short fantasy novellas with twists, The Empty Sky, Out of the Nowhere, and Whispers in the Dark are available now.

Twitter: https://twitter.com/KBElijah1
Instagram: https://www.instagram.com/k.b.elijah/

The Shadow
Chrissie Rohrman

Katie found the book at a secondhand bookstore and thought it was one of those novelty collector things. It had a gorgeous, deep-purple leather cover, and whisper-thin pages containing what looked to be handwritten spells.

"Come on," she said when I rolled my eyes. "It'll be fun."

We opened to a random page. *Conjuring a Passenger.* Katie thought it was a laugh-worthy riot the entire time she was reading.

Except, now I keep seeing this…shadow…everywhere I go.

I think Katie saw it first. She stopped being fun, then she stopped being everything else, too.

I'm scared that I'm next.

Chrissie Rohrman

Chrissie Rohrman is a training supervisor living in Indianapolis, Indiana with her husband and five fur babies. She enjoys white wine and writing competitions, and is currently drafting the first installment of a young adult fantasy trilogy. For publishing and writing updates, as well as general wonderings, follow her on Twitter @ChrissieRawrman, or 'like' Chrissie Rohrman Writes Things on Facebook.

The Siren's Symphony
EZ Whitney

The tip of her sharp, black nail carved into my collarbone, leaving ribbons of my skin to fall against the damp stone.

And as her composition grew, music notes dotting my breasts and curling around my ribs, the lines of the staff blurred as my blood seeped out.

I did not struggle.

I was both her easel and canvas, her palette and paint…I was muse, I was slave, I was parchment. And, for as long as her song played on, the gentle lilt of her voice forever ringing in my ears, my siren could do with me whatever she pleased.

EZ Whitney

A work-at-home mom with big dreams and an English degree, EZ Whitney writes romance, fantasy, and young adult novels in her limited spare time. To learn more about the author and her future works, follow her at @ezwhitney.writes on Instagram!

Clockmaker's Curse
N.M. Brown

Shana lifted her wedding skirts before climbing atop her husband. This would be the first time they were intimate since their wedding; she wanted to make it memorable. He'd already disrobed, except for the leather watch on his left hand.

Shana had never seen him without it.

She grabbed his wrist in the heights of ecstasy, shattering the watch's face as it slammed into the bedpost.

His face filled with horror as color drained from his body. His skin, some of which was still inside her, withered and fell away in dried flakes, leaving a mummified corpse in its wake.

Concrete Certainty
N.M. Brown

I pulled into my boyfriend's driveway, eager to present him with my freshly-manicured ring finger. He had asked me to marry him; in response I took the weekend to think. Not very romantic, I know, but there are things about me that most would find hard to accept.

My heart shattered as the living room window revealed another woman bobbing between his legs.

I embraced the long-feared feeling, allowing it free passage. A smile molded my lips as I saw their skin begin to calcify. Soon they were nothing more than a pornographic statue, about to be bashed into dust.

N.M. Brown

N.M. Brown is a happily married mother who sheds light on the dark corners of the mind that we like to keep hidden. She has stories in Sirens at Midnight, the recent award winning series Calls From the Brighter Futures Suicide Hotline, along with several others. Her passions include soap making, publishing and spending time with family.

Not a Witch
A.E. Hellstorm

Round and round rode the masked men on motorbikes. Some carried lit torches in hand; they had used them on the house since I refused to come out for a proper stake-burning. The roaring of the bikes matched the roaring of the fire. Through the flames that made my skin blister and crack, I saw the rats crawling through the open portal. Their eyes gleamed red as they waited for me to shred my human shell and become who I truly am.

"Not a witch, you fools," I laughed at the bikers and stepped out of my body, "a demon."

A.E. Hellstorm

A.E. Hellstorm was born in Sweden but spent her childhood in the mythology-rich soil of Greece. As an adult, she wanted to see more of the world and moved to Canada, pursuing a career in writing, photography, and graphic design. She is an award-winning author brimming with ideas, stories, and characters who hopes that she will be able to see them all in print one day.

Brackish Mistakes
Sherry Osborne

He stared into his empty scotch glass, the wind and rain battering the windows. He didn't have much time. He never should've abducted the mermaid who'd washed ashore, but his unabashed greed had overwhelmed him. He'd been blinded by the anticipation of slowly bleeding her of her magic, of transferring it to his own veins to give himself the powers he'd only ever dreamed of, but she was stronger.

Of course she was.

She would seek her revenge soon. Her escape was inevitable, and he'd killed off anyone who could have helped. The glass tank shattered behind him.

Game over.

Sherry Osborne

Sherry Osborne is a writer from Montreal, Quebec living in Halifax, Nova Scotia. She loves to read and write a variety of genres but has a passionate love of the horror genre. Being scared in real life is terrible – but being scared in a fictional world is invigorating and fun! She has written two novels and is in a cycle of revisions, querying, and writing new stories. One day she hopes to publish a long string of novels and will embarrass her children by screaming in public in a bookstore when she sees her own work on the shelves. Sherry lives in a constant state of "what if" and wishes she needed less sleep so she could write more.

She can be found at her sporadically updated website, http://sherryosborne.com and far too often on Twitter at http://twitter.com/busybooklife

The Alicanto Will Fly Again
Ximena Escobar

Casting its shadow like a dreadful mountain upon the other carcasses and skulls, the puma's jaw stood out amongst the mage's array of skeletal remains; seemingly alive in the waving orange reflections of his torch. The metallic shine of the ancient Alicanto rib was also easily recognizable; only remnant of the extinct raptor that he possessed. He observed it near the flame, its porousness; sparkling with particles of gold and silver within the bone, from all the precious minerals the raptor had ingested.

A puma ran across the desert, lifting a cloud of pearlescent dust. Soon he'd need his wings.

Three Three Three
Ximena Escobar

Three sets of bright eyes glowing.

Three words mumbled in the far corner of my blindness.

Three shadows towering.

Three hoods uncovering the unmeasurable darkness upon me.

See it descend.

See one raise the magic-imbued blade.

My flesh tears open before I can scream; a sizzling sound searing my lips shut.

Cupped hands rise, surging from the hollowed depths of my womb.

A black ball twitching—like the knowing void within me.

See its restlessness.

See the other sphere, where the Dark Lord watches.

See his bony hands clasp it.

Hear him say—clearly, ever so clearly—"Son of mine."

Kaida Steals The Show
Ximena Escobar

Kaida's eyes darkened when she saw the dancer, but only until she lit her torches; then her iris flared with flames of her own.

She looked away, unimpressed; but everyone else stared at her, especially Daniel—spellbound by her body, the spinning flames; the black mane fanning between the fire rings.

A blaze gushed out of Kaida's mouth. The fire consumed them—dancer breasts sunken like hollow mouths melting. Screams of horror erupted; but suddenly back in their forms, the pair could only join the enthused cheering.

Kaida left, her diabolo dragging in the sand.

Happy to steal the show.

Ximena Escobar

Ximena is writing short stories and poetry. Originally from Chile, she lives in Sydney with her family.

You can follow her progress on Facebook: @ximenautora

Inferno Tempest
G.L. Dalton

"Destroy him!"

The lord marshal shook the very foundations of the fortress as he bellowed the last command.

Lailoken, the grand mage, thrust his sceptre high into the air to bring forth the darkest powers at his command.

The blast of dark flame crashed against the prince in a blaze of black and purple waves.

He was engulfed entirely, his screams drowned out by the roar of the fire that enveloped him.

Blood exsanguinated from the body in a crimson cloud that pooled around his feet, the very flesh tearing away in bursts of navy fumes.

Then there was nothing.

G.L. Dalton

Having studied creative writing and media production at college, I was always drawn to screen an stage plays and have written several in the past with the intention of production. My passion for writing has been my main focus for several years now and during that time i have written many short stories and several science fiction novels. At this moment in time I am writing a 1980's spy thriller series as well as continuing work on a 6 novel series set in an expansive science fiction universe.

KIRIGAMI
Frances Lu-Pai Ippolito

"What color?" Shinu gestured to a rainbow of colored paper.

Head wrapped in a plastic bag, the man's pupils dwindled to tiny dots. The bag ends were tied around his neck, and the fog of his breath filled the inside.

"No preference then." Shinu shrugged.

Snip, slice, clip. She cut out a paper snake and balanced it on the shoulder of the unconscious man. One hand on the snake, and one on his forehead, she bound the man's soul to the paper fibers. She plucked up the twitching snake and dropped it upon her collection of a hundred paper animals.

PIANZI (IMPOSTOR)
Frances Lu-Pai Ippolito

"Your Majesty, the Crown Prince is here," Eunuch Tang said, nose to the ground.

"Again?" She unconsciously patted her towering headpiece, confirming to herself she looked the part of Empress Dowager.

"Mother, a present." A young man dressed in yellow silk embroidered with a phoenix and dragon entered the room.

A single horned, goat-like creature clomped in beside him. Its intelligent, black eyes watched the Empress.

"What's this?" She sipped her tea, wary of the animal.

"A *xiezhi*. It eats liars."

"Your mother is pleased."

Roaring, the animal charged the throne, clamping its sharp teeth on the shape-shifter's neck.

Frances Lu-Pai Ippolito

Frances Lu-Pai Ippolito is an emerging Chinese American writer in Portland, Oregon. When she's not spending time with her children in the outdoors, she's working on short stories with diverse characters in unusual situations of horror, sci-fi, fantasy, or whatever genre-bending she can get away with. Her stories have appeared in Nailed Magazine and HauntedMTL. Her work was also recently featured in the Ooligan Press Writers of Color Showcase 2020 in Portland, Oregon.

Malpha
D'mitri Blackwood

A maiden stood high like a monarch on her mountainside perch, surrounded by her children – not babes of pink flesh, rather the crows who roosted there. They took to the maiden like she was a god, and in many cases she was. Her word final. But she was silent, clasping a sickly juvenile to her bosom, decrepit and molting to white. A single tear rolls down her porcelain cheek as she raises her left hand, coddling the baby with the right.

"Cxël zurtai Amnheiţ," her voice whispered.

A curse for those who plotted against her daughter.

The crows took flight.

D'mitri Blackwood

D'mitri Blackwood has been perfecting his craft for over a decade, weaving tales from a land lost, and long forgotten.

F
I
S
H

Burning Anger
Chisto Healy

She watched the villagers tie her to the stake. She watched them stare, afraid, even though it was she they were about to murder.

She watched them, trembling as they lit their torches and shaking when they carried them to the kindling at her feet.

She watched them, terrified of being close to her even as the fire burned its way up her bare legs.

She closed her eyes and opened her mouth. The flames that had burned their way in were then purged, vomited furiously upon the frightened crowd as their fear was realized.

Their screams were like music.

The Sorceress
Chisto Healy

The man released his coughing wife. He stood and faced the robed woman before him, red hair flowing from her cloak. He was pointing.

"You're supposed to be some kind of sorceress!" he spit. "Now's your chance to prove it. My wife is sick. Look at her, she's dying! Use your magic!"

The cloaked woman brushed a loose strand of hair from her face and looked down at the woman, shivering from fever and choking.

Then she lifted her gaze and smiled at the husband.

"I already did."

Climax
Chisto Healy

This was the moment.

After a century of feuding the wizards and witches had finally united. After all the war and bloodshed they now found ecstasy in each other.

Julius, a master wizard, and Morrigon, queen of the witches, soared high above the land in all their nakedness, making love without a care for the world below. Their passion created lightning and storms, fires and floods. As the people screamed and died below them they moaned for each other.

When they reached simultaneous climax their magic blasted outward in a shockwave, burning in every direction until the world was gone.

Coming of Age
Chisto Healy

Jonathon stood amid the others, the boys that had kicked and punched him and the girls that had laughed about it. Through all the abuse he knew it was just a matter of time; it would come to him at sixteen, just like it did his father.

Jonathon had dreamed of this many times, and now it was finally here. His fingers curled and flicked, and the children watched in horror as the boys and girls next to them twisted, flopped and broke, smashing against the ceiling and floor. At the center of the classroom Jonathon smiled.

Best birthday ever.

The Wand
Chisto Healy

Byron looked down at the old woman before him, her body unmoving. "She's dead. What does she need it for?" he said. He picked up the wand that lay beside the corpse, a smile on his face. His smile faltered as the wand attached itself to him, turning his hand to wood.

His eyes bulged with horror as it kept going, crackling up his arm to his chest, neck and face. Byron's frozen scream became grains in the wood, the man-sized wand collapsing. It fired blue light at the dead body, and the old woman sat up with a smile.

Chisto Healy

Chisto Healy has been writing since childhood, but he only started following his dreams and writing full time in 2020. On top of the award nominated self published novels from his earlier days, he now has 80 published stories. You can find out what is out to read at his blog or follow him on Amazon as there is new stuff constantly coming out. He lives in NC with his fiance and her mom, his daughter Ella who has inspired stories that have been published, and his daughter Julia who has been published alongside him in this very book, and his son Boe who thinks the world is his drum. Blog https://chistohealy.blogspot.com

Ambition
Rich Rurshell

Since Ornella had already charmed Michael Campbell, the company's assistant director, the only people standing between her and her promotion now were Dane Griffiths and Jennifer, that bitch wife of his.

Watching through the waters of her font of vision Ornella grinned with glee as Dane stepped on the confusion hex runes outside his front door. She giggled as he picked up his son's baseball bat to fend off the knife-wielding maniac who came to greet him in the hallway. She gasped as Jennifer's body hit the floor. She called the police as Dane beat his wife to a pulp.

Rich Rurshell

Rich Rurshell is a short story writer from Suffolk, in the UK. His horror, Sci-Fi, and Fantasy stories explore the best and worst of what humanity, and the universe as a whole have to offer. When Rich is not writing stories, he enjoys music, film, and reading.

A Debt
Sophie Wagner

Returning from her day of hiking Mahika collapsed on her bed, feeling disoriented and weak. Reaching into her boot she pulled out a gemstone she had hidden there, although the guide had made it clear that you must never take anything from the forest in case it was cursed by fairies.

She took it nonetheless.

About to change her clothes, she noticed her body had started to wither and rot. Mahika screamed in horror. Suddenly her body began to convulse, causing her to collapse. The last thing she saw before darkness overtook was the stone glowing bright red.

Friends in Other Places
Sophie Wagner

Arelia slammed her door and grabbed her ouija board. She couldn't outright kill Evan for cheating on her. God wouldn't help her with that, but maybe someone on the Other Side would help?

She placed her hands on the board and loudly proclaimed, "If there is any spirit out there, help me get back at Evan!" Arelia didn't even wait for an answer; she took her hands off the board and went to lie down.

Arelia trusted the universe.

The next morning she awoke to a message written in blood on her wall.

We scratch your back, you scratch ours.

SOPHIE WAGNER

Sophie Wagner is an emerging student author from Ontario. She has been published by The Black Hare Press, For women Who Roar, Iron Faerie publishing and many more. She hopes that you have a horror filled day!

Changes
Katie Jordan

Alexander's icy breath hits Madison's neck, cooling the skin of her collarbone and causing goosebumps to rise.

He slides the sharp edges of his teeth across her throat. "You smell intoxicating."

"Just do it," Madison pleads, pressing her neck against his fangs.

In mere moments he will taste her warm blood. She wants him to, she wants to be his forever.

His teeth chomp down. He twists his jaw from side to side, allowing her to writhe in pain. As her eyes expand and the blood gurgles in her throat, she wonders if this is the beginning or the end.

Katie Jordan

Katie lives in the Pacific Northwest with her bonsai enthusiast husband, Brad, two daughters, and the world's loneliest goldfish seeking a friend, Fishy McFishfish. She dabbles in writing dystopian, fantasy, horror, sci-fi, and women's fiction.

Website: https://authorkatiejordan.com/

The Last King
Curtis A. Deeter

The alchemists danced in feral patterns to the rhythm of goatskin drums, cackling at their own shadows, and Cordelius shed his mantle for the last time.

She laid, sprawled in the caldera, body heaving, scales slimy, brittle, and peeling apart. A plume of black smoke sputtered to the ceiling.

Cordelius did not blame the alchemists, he blamed himself. *This could have been avoided, had we listened.* With his kingdom collapsing he was ready to die beside her: the last king with the last dragon.

"Easy, girl." She cooed and rubbed her snout against him. "We're going home now, to rest."

Curtis A. Deeter

Curtis A. Deeter is an author of fantasy, science fiction, and horror. When he is not writing, he enjoys spending time with his family, discovering new music, and taste-testing craft beer at local breweries.

Instagram: https://www.instagram.com/curtis_a._deeter/
Website: https://curtisadeeter.com/

Aviary
Marc Sorondo

The village children called her a witch; Thomas thought them cruel and stupid. She'd always been kind, gave him treats and showed him new birds.

Today she'd given him a tart filled with sweet custard.

"The soul is a bird." She led him through the aviary. "I picture yours as a bluebird…plumage like summer sky."

Thomas followed her.

"Let's see if I'm right."

When the spell hit him he felt the tart in his belly—hot and heavy as molten lead.

Then he felt light.

He looked down at himself.

She'd been wrong—his plumage was firey reds and oranges.

Of Smoke and Shadow
Marc Sorondo

She clutched the talisman in both trembling hands, holding it against her chest. If its enchantments couldn't protect her nothing could.

The first tendril slithered out of the dark, a serpentine shadow given substance. It reached out for her and she, muttering incantations, held out the amulet before her.

The tentacle, dark as a thundercloud, slithered out on the air. Its tip was sharp and glossy as an eagle's talon, and it prodded the protective charm.

When the bewitched emerald at its center cracked she knew all hope was lost. The shadow reached out again, this time for her heart.

Sacrament
Marc Sorondo

A number of ingredients were required: skull of a ram killed by a single stroke of a headsman's axe, tongue of a liar hung for a crime which he did not commit, ash from elm wood burned beneath the dark sky of a new moon.

The ritual had to be performed perfectly, every syllable of the chant pronounced correctly.

It had been so much work, but now—seeing his cloven-hooved child, glossy and slick with gore, new to the world and soon to be its end— the priest brought his bloody hands to his face and wept tears of joy.

Burning Man
Marc Sorondo

The Order of the Silver Moon trapped me in the flame on an undying candle…in a stupid Burning Man spell. They tricked me, trapped me, and, after years of diligence, forgot about me. I've lived lifetimes of fiery agony; they have grown old and died, and new generations have taken their place.

The old witches of the Order underestimated me, however. Even tortured in fire I've been reaching out. A weak will and a curious mind make for an easy target.

Even for a child, snuffing out a candle is a simple thing.

Now I'll make the witches pay.

The Devil's Work
Marc Sorondo

Samantha had all of the Master's major pieces. She owned "Red Leaves," his only painting. She owned both of his novels and the full script of his play, all handwritten on vellum pages and bound in human skin. She owned sheet music, a violin sonata so difficult people had died attempting to play it. She'd collected sculptures, carvings, even a wooden puzzle box.

She believed she lacked a single artifact.

Samantha gathered her entire collection and took her place at its center. She slit her throat and bled out, her talented soul, freed by her own hand, the final piece.

Marc Sorondo

Marc Sorondo lives with his wife and children in New York. He loves to read, and his interests range from fiction to comic books, physics to history, oceanography to cryptozoology, and just about everything in between. He's a perpetual student and occasional teacher. For more information, go to MarcSorondo.com.

The Citadel
Jacek Wilkos

The Legion of Darkness triumphed. After a long, gory battle the human city was conquered. The cadaver squad commander approached Valpurgius – The Great Necromancer – and bowed, awaiting orders.

"My Lord, what should we do with all the corpses?"

"We will use them to build the citadel."

"Reanimate and send to work, understood."

"No, you idiot!" Valpurgius thundered. "The bodies will be the part of the building, its outer walls."

"I don't quite understand."

"The sight of such construction will evoke fear in every army. Nobody will dare to attack us."

"And if somebody tries?"

"Then I will revive the citadel."

Jacek Wilkos

Jacek Wilkos is an engineer from Poland. He lives with his wife and two daughters in a beautiful city of Cracow. He is addicted to buying books, he loves black coffee, dark ambient music and riding his bike. He writes mostly micro and flash fiction in the horror genre. His fiction in Polish was published in Szortal, Drabble na niedzielę, Niedobre literki, Horror Online. In 2019 he started to translate his writing to English, and so far it was published in Drablr, Rune Bear, Sirens Call eZine, Trembling With Fear, and in numerous anthologies by Black Hare Press, Alien Buddha Press, Eerie River Publishing, Insignia Stories, Fantasia Divinity, Reanimated Writers Press, KJK publishing.

You can find more about his writing at:
https://www.facebook.com/Jacek.W.Wilkos/

The Hell Hound Cometh
Gordon Dunleavy

The beast arrives at midnight; Hell is open once again. It used to terrify me. I used to run, but not this time. This time I'll fight back.

The blood caked on the beast's snout glistens in the moonlight, showing its teeth. I'm done being scared.

I open the heavy book, family-owned for centuries, to find my spell, but it falls in the mud. My grandfather will kill me if I survive. After reading the first page my eyes connect with, the beast is gone, but a massive rat sits where the beast was.

I'm not quite sure what's worse.

Gordon Dunleavy

Gordon Dunleavy has been published by Scare Street, Ghost Orchid Press, and Raven & Drake Publishing. His stories for Scare Street and Ghost Orchid Press were part of an Amazon number one selling anthology. His Scare Street story is on Audible and being translated into two other languages. Gordon is finishing up his second novel. You can visit him at GordonDunleavy.com or on Twitter @Gordon_Dunleavy Come by and say hi!

THE EARLY BIRD CATCHES THE WYRM

Christian Boustead

The magnificent, imposing dragon lay resplendent on his golden hoard, an invitation for any assassin, and they obliged.

From the dark stabbed fire, lightning and arrows to smote the beast where he lay, but all failed.

Then, from the darkness emerged a trio of killers: a wizard clutching his staff, an archer his bow and a dagger-weilding woman in leathers.

The two men might have grabbed the treasure, but the woman did not let them. For, as they watched, she swelled and changed to a scaly form. Before the wizard could even cast a spell her withering flames engulfed them.

Christian Boustead

Christian Boustead is a blind author who lives in Hanley Staffordshire. Dragon Games, Book Two of The Wereding Chronicles is his most recent novel. He has also written: Awakening of Magic, Book One of The Wereding Chronicles and The Voice of Nature, a collection of poetry.

If you wish to learn more about Christian and his works then you might like to visit his website: www.christianboustead.com or find him on Twitter @csboustead

BLOOD MAGIC
David Green

Logain flopped to the floor, his body a massive bruise.

Damn my arrogance, he grimaced. He'd taken the contract to hunt down the infamous Goran, leader of the fighter's guild. Confident, Logain attacked: only to discover his magic useless against his quarry.

One option remained, but he couldn't get close.

Goran approached and lifted Logain from the floor.

A mistake.

Logain thrust his forehead into the man's nose. Goran snarled as claret exploded across the mage's brow.

"Ever hear what a mage can do with a drop of your blood?" Logain smiled.

Goran screamed as flames erupted from his throat.

TOO MUCH
David Green

Smoke billows across the battlefield. I scan the horizon and don't look down, not wanting the dead's lifeless stares to haunt my dreams.

My master, Morgan, is responsible for the carnage. He lit up like an exploding star; never have I seen such power. He scoured the enemy from the field.

I hear his laughter in the mist. Morgan's shape appears before me, and I see his shoulder shake. I kneel in front of him and gasp.

Blood streams out of the black pits which held his eyes.

"The magic proved too strong, Lara," Morgan raves. "I saw too much."

A MATTER OF CONCENTRATION

David Green

The human thinks he's won.

It isn't the first time one of these so-called wizards has summoned me. An unavoidable situation for my kind. The battle has only begun.

The human watches me beyond his magical barrier. This wizard's nervous stench fills my nostrils and sharpens my focus. I bare my fangs, and I sense the human's doubt.

"You're mine, demon," he snarls, sweat beading on his forehead.

I laugh, and his concentration dips. It's all I need.

Flexing my will the barrier explodes, and my jaws snap on the human's neck.

His fiery blood tastes sweet in my throat.

THEIR GOD'S REBIRTH
David Green

The smooth stone of the altar is cold against my back as I test my bonds. They're secure.

The other cultists step close, chanting as they surround me. They cast back their hoods and beseech the night sky. I see purples and yellows swirl in the black heavens, and a chill kisses my skin.

"Are you ready, my child?"

"Yes," I whisper.

The leader drives his dagger into my chest. I scream, writhing as he removes my beating heart. A presence floods into the wound, which seals behind it.

I'm no longer living, yet neither am I dead.

I'm more.

STOLEN GOODS
David Green

Finn ducked into a side-street. No one followed him, and he had the book.

Whatever you do, thief, don't open it. The mage commanded.

"Fuck that," Finn muttered, unlocking the book's clasp. "One wizard'll outbid another. Let's see what it's worth…"

Finn tried to scream, but only a strangled whimper escaped his throat. His eyes bulged at the page's secrets, blood leaking from his mouth as he chewed on his tongue.

Finn dropped the grimoire, smashing his head against the wall until it caved in and his vision failed.

Laying on the stones the book's cover closed with a snap.

DAVID GREEN

David Green is a writer based in Co Galway, Ireland. Growing up between there and Manchester, UK meant David rarely saw sunlight in his childhood, which has no doubt had an effect on his dark writings. Published by Red Cape Publishing, Eerie River Publishing, and many others. David has been nominated for the Pushcart Prize 2020 and has his debut dark fantasy series, In Soltiude's Shadow, releasing in June 2020.

Website: www.davidgreenwriter.com
Twitter: @davidgreenwrite

Bookworm

Laurence Sullivan

Retinal detachment. Medical emergency.
   The moment Luciano's mother heard these words she raced her boy to the hospital.

***

   The first specialist was bemused. Luciano had described seeing a black curtain drawing across his vision – but his retina looked firmly attached.
   Little Luciano revealed he had been reading just before it started. Well, *trying* to. The words failed to make sense to him, saying them out loud only formed garbled gibberish.
   Failing vision? Dysphasia? A neurological disorder?
   The truth was no medical department could cure an ancient incantation; nor diagnose the eldritch parasite that had already taken up residence within him…

First Born
Laurence Sullivan

The bull's heart hadn't worked. Ariel had tried drenching it in unguents and oils, but clearly they weren't enough.

It was the heart itself, it had to be – it must have been lacking some essential element that would bring her childhood doll to life.

Freshness? Not possible; the bull had been thriving in the field that morning.

Vitality? No. It had been difficult to take down alone; it resisted to its last breath.

Humanity.

A life for a life. The chance to cherish a child of her own – one born within the body of the doll she'd once so loved…

Laurence Sullivan

Runner-up in the Wicked Young Writer Awards: Gregory Maguire Award, Laurence Sullivan's creative writing has appeared in such places as: Londonist, The List, NHK World-Japan, Literary Orphans and Popshot Quarterly. He became inspired to start writing during his studies at the universities of Kent, Utrecht and Birmingham – after being saturated in all forms of literature from across the globe and enjoying every moment of it. He is currently pursuing a PhD at Northumbria University in the Medical Humanities, exploring literary portrayals of women's domestic medicine during the eighteenth century.

Website: www.laurencesullivan.co.uk

Solution-Oriented
Kimberly Rei

Modern life meant modern problems. Odette stood on her balcony looking out over the city, the wind whipping black hair into a tangle. A full moon hung low. Lights flickered on and off, thousands going about their lives.

She smiled as a feathered creature, born of nightmares, landed on the railing. She held out a hand, barely wincing as it pecked at her finger and licked the wound.

"Deliver my message, beloved. Be sure it is understood."

As the beast took wing she sipped a bourbon. The old ways demanded blood. Flesh. Her pet would gather both, in vast quantities.

Caught Between
Kimberly Rei

The most powerful of magics coursed through his veins. He plotted carefully, waiting for the day he would break free and exact his revenge.

All around him, as far as he could see, stood stone statues. Every one of them, man and creature alike, looked startled. Granite hid the terror he knew writhed beneath the surface.

His fingertips sparked. He felt it; his power was returning...or he was losing more feeling. Salvation or damnation, with no way to discern the difference.

Medusa slithered past, spiking his hatred.

He'd have his vengeance, as soon as he was flesh once more.

The Music of Life
Kimberly Rei

Plucked petals fell to the floor, each becoming a claret, drop-shaped gem. They crafted musical notes as they struck worn stone, the small workshop filling with ethereal tones as the hag worked. It was the one mark of beauty in her world.

She gathered the stones, savouring the power pulsing stronger as they grouped together. She would make jewelry of them. She would slip them into poppets. She would transcend them.

A whimper drew her attention, spoiling her mood. She lashed out with a willow stick, slashing the dangling body.

Blood fell, turning to ruby petals, turning to claret gems.

On the Night of the Fifth Moon
Kimberly Rei

The conclave of magi met annually on the Fifth Moon, as they had for millennia. Each had a clear memory of the First Meeting. Shared memory, not stories told to children. Tonight they were welcoming a new member; blood sacrifice was required.

He was scared, they all had been. His ears twitched, panicked. His black, button nose wrinkling as he sneezed. Nerves. One never knew how they would take hold.

The rite was swift. In moments the gushing ankle was bandaged. He would heal. Forgive. His soft paw would join the others strung across the glade.

A lucky place indeed.

Kimberly Rei

Kimberly Rei does her best work in the places that can't exist... the in-between places where imagination defies reality.

Her debut novelette, Chrysalis, is available on Amazon (https://readerlinks.com/l/1416028).

Always on the lookout for new ideas, new projects, and new ways to make words dance, Kim is happiest behind a keyboard or doing anything at all with her beautiful wife.

Full-Moon Vengeance
Nicole Honl

Overwhelming rage was all she knew. If the ignorant peasants wanted to act like a pack of wolves, hunting down her kind, then she would make them wolves.

Hair from a mother wolf, blood from a human male, a single petal from a Queen of the Night bloom - all difficult to acquire, but not as difficult as the incantation would be to speak.

She would witness their doom and listen to their howling cries if it was the last thing she did. Only then would she be able find solace In the fact that their lives were ruined like hers.

Family Secrets
Nicole Honl

I pause in descent down the stairs, my heart beating wildly. The lupus curet is choking itself on the metal collar around its throat, pulling as hard as it can against the chain that keeps it confined to this basement. It doesn't feel the pain of its change, and rushes again and again at me as hard as it can.

Half of its human skin has already fallen off, and it claws at me with its one transformed arm; it wants to kill everything in its path. I race back up the stairs, wanting to rid myself of this secret.

A Different Kind of Genie
Nicole Honl

When I wake the bloody, disemboweled bodies of my fellow explorers lay at my feet. Fear freezes me in this wretched place.

Splat.

Splat.

Splat.

I look down and immediately drop the dagger in my hands. The dagger that originally drew me in now glows an eerie red, as if the sacrifice before me imbues it with power.

"What have I done?" I whisper.

"You have given me life," a male voice echoes throughout the pyramid halls.

"I…" I lift my shaking hands to see them coated red with the blood of my friends. "What have I done?" I cry.

Nicole Honl

Nicole Honl lives in Minnesota with her husband and multiple fur-babies. She works full time as an accountant but spends the majority of her free time either writing or reading. To follow Nicole, see her LinkTree at https://linktr.ee/Nicole_Honl

Wrathful as Roses
Sarah Matthews

Vivianne was a witch who could control plants— a Floramancer.

She lived in a tiny cottage surrounded by beautiful flowers, shrubs and succulents. Her neighbors admired and respected her verdant garden, but her mailman was another story.

"You've trampled my roses for the last time!" she yelled.

The mailman tried to stammer an apology, but with a wave of Vivianne's hand thick, thorny tendrils exploded from the ground and snaked towards the frightened mailman. They wrapped themselves around him, pulling him into the earth.

Vivianne would set him free in a minute, but it was the principle of the matter.

Ignatio's Calling
Sarah Matthews

A raven flapped its way through the window of an ancient stone tower. It alighted on a wooden table full of arcane artifacts. Its black eyes gleamed with more than avian intelligence.

"Ignatio, tell me, what did you observe?" asked the sorceress.

"Treason. Treachery. Betrayal," croaked Ignatio.

"Good," she said. "I was hoping to get a chance to use this again." She pulled out a double-headed axe that glowed a baleful, bloody red. "Rally my undead army," she commanded. "We attack tonight."

Ignatio cawed and ruffled his wings, then flew off through the midnight sky to complete his mistress's will.

The Audition
Sarah Matthews

The rogue wizard known as Pentagram Jim greeted me with a tip of his top hat and a loin-stirring smirk.

"Show me your powers," I said.

He nodded. "Gladly."

Rolling up his sleeves to reveal interwoven pentagram tattoos on his arms, he then gesticulated fiercely at a passing man.

The man was turned inside-out into a raw, glistening mass of flesh. Such a disgusting and fascinating sight to behold! I saw his brain, I think, before Pentagram Jim set him right. The man ran off, shrieking hysterically.

"Do I get the job then?" asked Pentagram Jim.

I smiled. "You're hired."

The Sacrifice's Revenge
Sarah Matthews

"Hecate, hear my plea! Enhance my powers beyond those of any sorcerer, living or dead!" I cried.

I raised my knife to the goat's throat, ready to sacrifice it, but before I could strike the candles around the altar guttered and went out. In the darkness a pair of red eyes gleamed.

With a word I relit the candles, their glow illuminating dozens of goats. Behind them rose a horned figure in tattered robes.

"You will harm my children no more," it growled. I let go of the goat, who ran off to join its brethren.

"Hecate, hear my pleas…"

The Un-Familiar
Sarah Matthews

The wizened wizard addressed his colleagues at the Sorcery Symposium.

"Behold! In this cage I have a Great Horned Carrionbird. They are immortal, and possess immense intelligence. I intend to switch souls with it so that I may never die, and it shall serve me as a human familiar. Observe!"

Uttering guttural words in an ancient language he pointed his wand at the bird. Both man and bird collapsed. When the wizard arose he screamed piteously, then bashed his head against the wall until he was dead.

"Well, fuck," croaked the Carrionbird. "Can someone let me out of this cage?"

SARAH MATTHEWS

Sarah Matthews is a writer of horror/fantasy/humor from New Albany, Indiana. She has been published recently in Forgotten Ones from Eerie River Publishing. Follow her on Twitter @superbfinch.

The Unquiet Dead
J. A. Skelton

The birds fell silent when he stepped into the forest; the shadow prince with eyes as fierce as a god's wrath.

The wind stilled around him as he lifted his hands to the whispering leaves and called upon the creatures that slumbered below. The unquiet dead; those unearthly bodies that slept deep beneath the soil in a labyrinth of bones and teeth.

With a sound like creaking wood and ancient thunder the ground opened into a great maw of darkness.

A pale, rotting hand reached out from the shadows, and with a smile like silver thorns the prince took it.

The Witch's Dance
J. A. Skelton

They danced beneath the waxen moon, wearing the skins of the old gods on their backs.

The fire burned like the Devil's breath, scorching the edges of the sky and turning the ground black with ash.

The witches screamed and howled in the tongues of their ancient ancestors, raising their heads to the bone-white moon and whispering their secrets to the stars.

The fire began to twist and writhe like a living thing, devouring the taste of blood and magic in the air as red embers drifted to the ground like falling stars.

The Gods would be reborn this night.

The Old Ones
J. A. Skelton

The wind chimes sang, but there was no wind.

There was something else in the air, something like the hungry tides and the wild mountains; something as old and wise as time itself.

Elijah opened the window and let the darkness creep inside, his name on its breath.

They were waking from their slumber, from deep below the chasm of the earth, and he was being summoned to battle once more.

The ground split asunder. They rose in a torrent of fire and fury, turning the sky the color of blood and eclipsing the sun.

The Old Ones had returned.

J. A. Skelton

J. A. Skelton is a UK-based writer of horror fiction. When she's not working on her freelance business or studying for university, she spends her time writing ghost stories and going for long walks in the woods. Her favourite writers include Daphne Du Maurier, Shirley Jackson and Susan Hill. She currently has stories submitted in two horror anthologies, and is looking forward to getting more of her work out into the public eye.

Gone with the Waves
Radar DeBoard

Tilithos moved his hands up with trembling ferocity, the waves of the sea rising with the kinetic energy he willed into them. He put all his energy forth and sent the waves higher and higher.

With one final push he sent the waves over the walls of Kalto Bernton. The ocean water washed through the streets, sweeping up helpless citizens as it went. Tilithos listened to the screams of thousands of people. He waited until the city was silent, then allowed the water to drain. He smiled as he made his way to the steps of his new castle.

Lyphus' Army
Radar DeBoard

"This madness ends, Lyphus!" Sir Gerod loudly exclaimed while drawing his sword. "Whatever army you were hoping to create won't happen!"

Lyphus raised an eyebrow, "Oh really? I suppose the king didn't tell you exactly what kind of sorcerer I am."

"Who cares!?" Gerod shouted, "That doesn't matter now, because I have you cornered."

Lyphus smiled as he watched the pile of bones behind Gerod slowly stand up. The skeleton produced a sword and stabbed it directly through the gut of Sir Gerod.

Lyphus shook his head, "A valiant effort." He smiled, "You'll make a fine addition to my ranks."

Armored Protector
Radar DeBoard

The blade pierced into the thief's abdomen with ease. The armored glove slowly pulled back the handle of the sword, inflicting maximum pain. Once the sword was fully withdrawn the thief collapsed, then gasped his last breaths before passing away.

The suit of animated armor bent down and picked up the chalice that lay on the floor, carefully placing it back on the altar. With its duty complete it moved back to its spot, standing tall and still behind the altar. It gave one final look out at the several dispatched bodies strewn across the ground before going completely motionless.

Ozildor's Retribution
Radar DeBoard

Ozildor waved his arms one final time as he finished reciting the last bit of the spell. He looked out from his high tower over the kingdom of Voupponid.

He reflected on the centuries of service he had provided for the royal court; there was no issue of the past two hundred years that Ozildor did not have a hand in resolving. That is, until the king banished him for a simple reanimation spell.

The king had disrespected Ozildor by casting him out, so punishment had to come. Ozildor smiled as the gigantic balls of fire fell from the sky.

Azothor's New Spell
Radar DeBoard

Henrick smiled at Azothor as she led him to the stables. She quietly shut the door behind them as they entered.

"So, what is it you wanted to show me?" Henrick asked.

"I learned a new spell," Azothor replied. She began to chant as energy built up in her fingers. Henrick watched as Azothor's hands glowed red with energy, a sinister grin spreading across her face just before she unleashed the energy at Henrick. In a matter of seconds his flesh was burnt away, leaving a pile of bones behind.

Azothor laughed, "That's what you get for calling magic dumb."

Radar DeBoard

Radar is a horror movie and novel enthusiast who resides in Wichita, Kansas. He occasionally dabbles in writing and enjoys to make dark and exciting tales for people to enjoy. He has had drabbles and short stories published in various electronic magazines and anthologies.

Links: https://www.facebook.com/WriterRadarDeBoard/
https://www.goodreads.com/author/show/19676011.Radar_DeBoard

The Proof
Andrew Kurtz

"It is impossible to raise the dead," the goblin informed the wizard.

"Not so. A combination of dragon blood, elf urine and a few words from the ancient grimoire are all that are required," answered the wizard.

"Can you prove this nonsense?" challenged the goblin.

Upon hearing this the wizard thrust his dagger into the goblin's heart, immediately killing him. Afterwards he chanted a passage from the grimoire while applying the necessary ingredients.

The wizard walked away with a smile on his face, a bone-chilling scream filling the air as the goblin painfully returned to the land of the living.

The Will of the Storm
Clint Foster

Over the roar of the storm Fyeldi screamed, "Bring your thunder and lightning, and see both fail you!" She raised the dagger overhead, "Your minions cannot bind my hands as they once bound my thoughts."

The voice of the storm replied with a rolling boom.

She smiled, stabbed and removed the wet steel from her own breast. Yet even as the weapon left her body the wound it made closed, and no blood so much as stained her shirt.

If thunder could laugh it did, and she fell to her knees - doomed to eternity by a storm she once loved.

No Second Chances
Clint Foster

"Next."

The warlock bowed his head in shame, the king scarcely acknowledging him, too intent upon the twitching mess of bones and boiled flesh that pulsated in front of him. The best minds of a hundred kingdoms had competed for the chance to resurrect the queen. Yet, in spite of their proclamations of promises and miracles already worked, it was this which had been wrought by them.

With a nod a kingsguard tied the warlock's wrists and heaved him bodily into a waiting cauldron. The logs crackled softly, and the hiss of his skin was drowned by his screams.

"Next."

Clint Foster

Clint Foster lives with his herd of four cats and his wonderful wife, Nik, in southern Iowa. He has dozens of short stories published across a breadth of publishers, a novel, and an epic poem. He loves telling stories and always hopes others enjoy reading them.

Escape
Michael D. Nadeau

Footsteps drew his attention as he called upon the dark power within him. Caer knew that, if he had any chance of surviving, he had to strike first. The elf turned the corner and Caer let the power go, the black tendrils boring through the leathers of the guard; blood sprayed everywhere.

Caer laughed as he ran. Seeing the door to the dungeon he rushed forward, opening it and fleeing, feeling the sunlight beaming down on his tusks. Caer had escaped imprisonment, and would take his revenge upon the elves by leading his orcs back here and unleashing his power.

The Warlocks Charge
Michael D. Nadeau

The orcs swarmed over the walls and battered gates, cries of hatred and outrage on their tusks. Never again would the elves oppress or imprison them.

The orc warlock Caer led the charge, his deep voice intoning dark powers and driving fear into the elves. Blood dripped from his tusks as his spells claimed elven souls, and soon it was over; only the sounds of the dead and dying reached him.

"We secured the general, Caer," one female orc said as she came up with a struggling elf.

Caer spoke deeply, and darkness drained the elf. "We don't need him."

Death of the Queen
Michael D. Nadeau

Screams of pain and rage filtered through the halls of the ancient castle, reaching the elven queen on her throne of ivory. The orcs had come at last, fighting off the elves' slavery with dark powers. The prophecy said she couldn't die, unless an orc wielding dark magic assailed her castle.

That day seemed close indeed.

The doors caved in, the guards dying as black tendrils tore them apart, spraying the walls with blood.

An orc approached, dark fire burning in his eyes. "Your day has come at last, bitch queen. My name is Caer, and I am your death."

The Rite
Michael D. Nadeau

The moon was in alignment, and Sierra smiled as the crowd gathered at the stone dais. It was the night of her ascension when she would become the Sorceress of Havar. She gathered her silver dagger, cloth and bowl, smiling at her loving husband.

"Are you ready, my love?" her husband asked softly.

"Yes, thank you." She put the cloth around her neck and raised the dagger high above his prone, bound body, plunging it into his chest with force. As the moon shone through the clouds his blood pooled into rivulets, angling towards the bowl; it was done.

The Familiar
Michael D. Nadeau

The old man stumbled and cast again, the magic enveloping his enemy in flame. He had never thought they would come for him, yet he should've known they could never accept his familiar and the power it gave him.

"Are you alright, Master?" the tiny voice asked on his shoulder.

He reached up and ran his fingers through the child's hair as it clung to his neck. It was just the upper part of a three-year-old girl, bound to him by magic, but the power it had was immense. "Yes Lina, thank you. Your attachment is growing stronger each day."

Michael D. Nadeau

Born in the usual way, author Michael D. Nadeau found fantasy at the age of eight with Dungeons & Dragons. He is the author of the Lythinall series: The Darkness Returns book 1, The Darkness Within book 2, The Darkness Falls (coming soon), and Tales from Lythinall — an anthology (coming soon). He also has several stories in Eerie River Publishing anthologies, as well as writing for Gestalt Media.

Social Media Links
My Amazon: Amazon.com/author/karsis_the_bard
My Website: https://karsisthebard.wordpress.com/
My Twitter: https://twitter.com/Salen_Valari

La Venganza
C. Marry Hultman

The sounds of bullets and screams echoed outside. Juanita climbed into the bed, hugging her abuela's rigid form. The wrinkled body was still and cold. Shouts and heavy footsteps came closer. She closed her eyes as her mother called for help, followed by a gunshot.

The bedroom door opened, extinguishing the candles. A familiar figure entered.

"Come, mija."

"No!"

"I won't hurt you."

"You hurt Mama."

"Come here, little bitch."

The candles flickered to life as his screams cut through the night, his limp body crashing through the barred window.

The tranquil face of her abuela now bore a smile.

Few Return
C. Marry Hultman

They had trampled through Kaetil's sanctuary, through her beloved woods. Humans had pulled up ancient moss, carved names into trees and urinated in the creek.

Their reckless behavior enraged her. She turned to the shrine, sliced her gnarled hand and smeared the graven idol with her black blood.

The skies darkened, mist rolled in and the foxes let out their eerie calls. Kaetil watched as the frightened humans huddled together when lightning crackled overhead. She released the purple river crystals from her palm and watched as the spell enveloped them, erasing their minds.

Here they would remain, forever her playthings.

C. Marry Hultman

C. Marry Hultman is a teacher, writer and sometimes podcaster who is equal parts Swede and Wisconsinite. He lives with his wife and two daughters and runs W.A.R.G –The Guild podcast dedicated to interviewing authors about their creative process. In addition to that, he runs the website Wisconsin Noir – Cosmic Horror set in the Dairy State where he collects short fiction and general thoughts.

Find out more about him at https://linktr.ee/C.MarryHultman

Vengeance
Al Provance

Blood ran through hastily-carved dirt grooves towards a pool in the town center. It bubbled of its own accord, with no fire to heat it and none needed. Five families had lived in this village, and now thirty-two bodies poured the remains of their lives into the grisly whorls running through the street.

A young woman and her grandmother still stood, looking at the glow on the horizon. "They would kill us anyway, and not as quickly," the grandmother rasped. "Come, child, finish the ceremony that will bring the plague upon our enemies. Our swift death buys us exquisite revenge."

Al Provance

Al lives in southern New Hampshire with his wife and two children, where he teaches full time, and writes stories when he can.

Morrigan's Gift
R. S. Pyne

The tree stood black against the darkening sky, close to the place a cursed sorcerer fought and lost his last battle. His ending ensured nothing else grew; yet the tree still scraped a living, bare of leaves now as the land descended into winter.

Branches spread over a wrapped bundle laid among the age twisted roots. A newborn baby left to die – nobody to hear its cries except the uncaring scavenger birds. A raven's harsh call brought the Morrigan there instead. She called the child's spirit back long enough to grant vengeance against those who never gave it a chance.

Wood Witch
R. S. Pyne

Even Fair People would not dance on such a night, their circles standing empty while darker spirits roamed abroad. Wind howled through ancient trees, blowing over a cabin and a newly dug grave. Inside the old woman's fire burnt still lower.

Voices called her name in honeyed tones, but only death waited when the Blood Moon bathed the forest in crimson light. She spoke the words of an older magic, then saw the world through newly-born eyes. One last ritual remained – giving her old body back to the earth so the new one could run sky-clad along the secret trails.

R. S. Pyne

R. S. Pyne is a Welsh speculative fiction writer and mental health first aider. Fiction has appeared in Mad Scientist Journal, Aurora Wolf, Bete Noire, Albedo One, Bards and Sages Quarterly and elsewhere.

Forbidden Powers
Lauren Raybould

Enna's body pulsated, a glow emanating from her lithe body; her draconic powers were awakening.

"Go, now, before they kill you," her mother screamed as the doors blasted open. "I'll deal with them."

With one last look back at her mother, who was facing three guards, she leaped through the window, glass shattering. Outside, the silver dragon was waiting.

"What's happening to me?" Enna eyed her glowing hands.

"Your forbidden powers are awakening, child," a deep rumble came from the dragon's throat. "You must control them before they destroy you. Run, child — to the surface lands. Preserve our bloodline."

Lauren Raybould

Lauren is a freelance journalist and editor who is the owner of The Night Owl Editing and Copywriting, and provides editing, proofreading and copywriting services to indie authors, publishers and businesses.

When she's not working, she either has her head in a book, walking her dogs, playing video games, or going to music gigs and writing about them.

ASHES OF THE GRIMOIRE
Warren Benedetto

Neve poured the ashes of their mother's grimoire into the bowl. Larissa added a shimmering, crimson liquid, whispering incantations as she stirred.

The ashes congealed into clay, which Larissa sculpted into a small, human-like form; a homunculus. She pressed in pieces of volcanic glass where the eyes should be.

The eyelids opened.

"Hello, little one," Larissa whispered.

The homunculus smiled, revealing rows of pin-sharp teeth.

"Oh, he's precious!" Neve squealed as the homunculus climbed into her outstretched palm.

With a nod from Larissa the homunculus leapt, sinking its razored claws into Neve's eyes.

"Yes," Larissa said. "He is."

THE GIRL STEPPED AWAY FROM THE WINDOW

Warren Benedetto

The girl stepped away from the window, backwards.

Outside the flames consuming the village retreated, the smoke and fire drawn in through thatched rooftops. Shattered glass lifted from the ground, then assembled into panes that filled the empty windows. Broken bodies rose from the streets, their wounds closing and healing.

The girl sat on the bed, then lay down on the pillow. Her blanket slid soundlessly up from the floor, covering her. Her eyes closed.

In the town square the magus exhaled. He closed his ancient spellbook. The destruction the girl had wrought had been reversed, at least for now.

Warren Benedetto

Warren Benedetto writes short fiction about horrible people doing horrible things. He studied Evolutionary Biology at Cornell University, and has a Master's degree in Film/TV Writing from the University of Southern California. When he's not writing, he works as Director of Global Product Strategy at PlayStation, where he holds almost 20 patents for various types of gaming technology. He is also the developer of StayFocusd, the world's most popular anti-procrastination app for writers. He built it while procrastinating. For more information, visit www.warrenbenedetto.com, or follow @warrenbenedetto on Twitter.

Empty and Drawn
R. H. Newfield

Her bones and skin stretched unnaturally as she stood. The room was filled with the bodies of robed men, all laying dead along a painted circle, the center of which was where she stood. Nothing, not a memory or thought, came to her mind, only an insatiable hunger. She looked at the bodies, drool hanging at the corner of her mouth. Somehow, instinctually perhaps, she knew they couldn't quell her hunger.

She shambled out of the room into the city beyond. Countless divine lights dotted her vision. Unknowingly she smiled, a growl between her teeth. Hunger wouldn't be a problem.

More Than Dust
R. H. Newfield

A wind had picked up, drawing a sandstorm that stretched for miles. Despite the impending impact they all stood in their circle; mouths agape, bodies paralyzed. Before them was a great shadow slinking in the storm, significantly larger than the mountains. They had prayed, they had sacrificed, and now they had been rewarded.

But this wasn't what they expected, this wasn't what they knew.

A maw stretched out of the storm and grasped a nearby mountain, devouring it in mere seconds. There they stood, grains of sand to the approaching storm, unable to move as pure terror washed over them.

Murmurations
R. H. Newfield

Drawn by the whispers of hidden wizards It came in response. It arrived in a flurry of beating wings, a dark cloud shifting in shape. At first the town thought It was migrating birds, but with each undulating wave of the flock a single shadow kept Its place.

The town was whipped into a frenzy the closer It got, save for a select few in pitch-black robes; the backs of which were stylized as tattered, broken wings. They dropped to the floor in adoration as It approached, but the being cared not and the flock devoured them all the same.

R. H. Newfield

Ryan is a 28 year-old writer hailing from New York. For all of his life, Ryan was absolutely terrified of anything horror. Halloween was a holiday for staying indoors, movies were a source of his nightmares, and even the trailers of such left him sleepless. And yet, he was drawn into the world of written horror, seeking to combine it with the powerful nature of fantasy. The dread, the questions, the unknowable knowledge of horror combined with the magic, the hope, and the adventure of fantasy was far too alluring and fun.

https://twitter.com/rhuntern
https://www.youtube.com/RyanNewfield

Commuted Sentence
Peter J. Foote

"Yilf, drop the rope there," the Sorceress said, pointing at the base of the massive oak.

"Sorceress, when will my toil end? You said my labors would set me free."

"Soon Yilf, this is your last task. You have been diligent, gathering the ingredients for my summoning. Now you'll provide the last."

Panic replaced the confusion on Yilf's face.

"Blood from a hanged man, the last ingredient." The Sorceress smiled and cast her spell.

The rope animated, lashing out at Yilf and dragging him high into the oak's branches.

Once the body stopped thrashing the Sorceress smiled, drawing her blade.

Blood Bird
Peter J. Foote

The King observed the battlefield, grimacing.

"Demons are slaughtering our warriors, and if we're defeated here we lose our kingdom. Release the Blood Bird."

"Your Grace, the soldiers…!"

"Each knew the risk."

Servants brought the golden cage to the battlefield, lifting the latch. Freed, the Blood Bird leapt into the sky, blood dripping from its talons as it soared.

Crimson drops splattered the warriors, their eyes glowing red and battle madness filling their souls.

Ignoring mortal wounds they pushed the demons back, winning the day.

The soldiers touched by the Blood Bird collapsed, the dark magic holding them together spent.

Thirst
Peter J. Foote

"King Ansen! We beg you, throw down that sword," the guard shouted into the cave.

The crazed king stumbled from the shadows. A tarnished crown hid his eyes, regal robes shredded to rags and white knuckles gripping the blood-stained sword.

Ansen spoke through cracked lips. "I'd drop it, if I could. This blade thirsts for blood. It won't release me, I'm cursed."

"My king, please! We don't want this fight, but we must take you back." Guards drew steel, encircling their cursed king.

"Fools! Don't you realize the sword wants this?" The shattered king lifted the cursed blade and charged.

Peter J. Foote

Peter J. Foote is a bestselling speculative fiction writer from Nova Scotia, Canada. He runs the Fictionfirst Used Books, specializing in fantasy & sci-fi titles. He also cosplays with his wife, and alternates between red wine and coffee as the mood demands.

Many of Peter's stories reflect his personal life, as he is a firm believer in the adage that a writer should write what they know.

In total, Peter has been featured in over two dozen publications, with an interest in his short fiction worldwide.

As the founder of the group "Genre Writers of Atlantic Canada", Peter believes that the writing community is stronger when it works together.

Facebook: https://www.facebook.com/peterjfooteauthor
Twitter: https://twitter.com/PeterJFoote1
Website: https://peterjfooteauthor.wordpress.com/

Hag-Ridden
J. David Reed

I had learned the term at school, *hag-ridden*. Mum said it was an old term from back when witches and women of dark magic plagued the streets at night, sitting on sinners and making their dreams turn dark. *"We don't call 'em tha' anymore,"* she had chuckled as she smoothed out the bedspread and kissed my cheek.

It made me wonder what I'd done, then, to incite the woman who crushed my chest every night: her bulging eyes drinking my pain, her talons in my hair and her bony hips and knees bruising my ribs.

"Now we call 'em nightmares."

J. David Reed

J. David Reed is a working-class science-fiction and fantasy writer from the North of England, most recently published in the independent anthology series Little Book of Fairytales, by Dancing Bear Books.

With a BA(hons) in Scriptwriting and Drama, J. David is a lover of the dramatic and human, with a focus on stories that eschew a grand overblown scale to focus on the people within them. He is also a qualified teacher, and is passionate about making stories that are accessible for all audiences without sacrificing their meaning.

Another Execution
Jacqueline Moran Meyer

I cursed the crowd while being dragged to the gallows.

Four men held down my writhing body. As punishment for my refusal to exchange certain favors for mind-numbing wine, they placed the back of my neck on the stained stone.

I stared up at my executioner.

He struck.

My head rolled.

Cheers turned to screams when fire shot out of every pore of my shuddering body. While my tormenters burned I collected my head, propping it back on my lovely neck. I walked out of that town as I have so many towns before and will, no doubt, do again.

Hearts of Stone
Jacqueline Moran Meyer

"Do you suffer, sister?"

I did not respond, but my eyes, the only part of my body not yet turned to stone, expressed my torment.

"Good," Marcus smirked.

After our parents' death I fought my brother to rule the kingdom.

I lost.

Marcus placed a spell on me, turning me slowly to stone. He has visited me once a year for over fifty years to gloat over his victory.

I killed my parents and tortured their followers with ease all those years ago. No one had suspected what I had long planned, except for Marcus. He was ready, and armed.

Jacqueline Moran Meyer

JACQUELINE MORAN MEYER is a writer, artist and small business owner living in New York, where she received her master's degree from Teachers College, Columbia University. Jacqueline enjoys writing dark speculative fiction. Her favorite author is Alice Munro and her favorite film…is…anything horror related. Jacqueline also enjoys hiking with her dog Molly and the company of her husband Bruce and daughters; Julia, Emma and Lauren.

Website: www.jmoranmeyer.net
Amazon: amazon.com/author/jacquelinemoranmeyer
Twitter: @jmmeyer64

Her Black Wings
Joshua Borgmann

My angel opened the door and greeted me with a hug. I put my donation on the dresser. Brushing against her softness, I felt the wings concealed under her shear slip.

"Thank you, sweetie," she said as she counted out the $500.

"That's just a starter," I said. "I want you to take everything this time."

"Everything?"

She slipped off her heels.

"My life, and my soul."

I sensed sadness in her silver eyes as we undressed.

"I love you," she whispered as she mounted me. Those gorgeous, black wings filled my vision as she lovingly rocked me toward oblivion.

Joshua E. Borgmann

Joshua E. Borgmann holds degrees from Drake University, Iowa State University, and the University of South Carolina. He grew up on horror and science-fiction and had long intended to become a great master of the art form before he was sucked into the bottomless pit of academia. He toils away his days as an English instructor at a small community college and dreams of being able to escape into a world of fantasy and terror where there are no student papers to grade. He resides in a nameless rural Iowa town surrounded by terrible cornfields.

LAST LETTER
Daniel Loring Keating

For the third night in a row the army of ghouls has come. The city's knights and archers, exhausted from the previous two nights of combat, have been defeated and overrun.

The ghouls scream in an ancient tongue unknowable by the living. They are slaughtering men, women and children in the streets. The roads run red with their blood. They will start in on the houses soon. I have only my little iron dagger, a ward against sneaking thieves rather than an implement of war.

Miriam, if you read this know that I love you. Tell our son the same.

Daniel Loring Keating

Daniel Loring Keating grew up in post-Industrial New England, where he earned a BA in Creative Writing from Chester College of New England. He has an MFA in Creative Writing at the California College of the Arts, where he was the Managing Editor of Eleven Eleven Journal. His speculative work has appeared in the Hawk & Cleaver horror podcast, The Other Stories, the JayHenge Publishing anthology, Sensory Perceptions, and the Rogue Blades Entertainment anthology, Death's Sting.

An Offering
Scott McGregor

Koisa completed the ink-drawn symbol of a Balor's face. The sorceress watched closely, captivated by the princess' ruthless desire. Then Koisa positioned the tied-up boy at the center of the marked Balor, no older than ten, and in Koisa's hand twirled a dagger.

Finally, the sorceress spoke up.

"An offering of blood must be made to achieve the power you seek, Princess."

Koisa pressed the blade against her brother's throat. "If blood is required, then it shall be paid."

Crimson washed over the marking, and the sorceress chanted the abyssal spell.

The following day Koisa reigned as Queen of Arcis.

The Black Flames
Scott McGregor

From within my bedroom I watched the world blaze, slowly devoured by ferocious black fire. Clouds of smoke painted the sky for miles, the heat creeping inwards.

The worst part? This was all my fault.

On my desk rested my notebook, propped open to the page that contained the conclusion of the dark fantasy novel I recently finished writing.

…the embers raged on, and the black flames of Valen consumed a million souls across the land until nothing but ash remained.

The End.

Mother always said my stories were magical, but I never understood why until it was too late.

Mother Dearest
Scott McGregor

On a cold night in Yarhelm Carol dragged her daughter Suzy to the well on the outskirts of town. In her hand she held a bottle of slithering centipedes.

"Momma, please!" Suzy begged.

"Forgive me, Suzy." With garden shears Carol sliced her daughter in half. She dumped her remains, followed by the centipedes, down the well, then Carol chanted a passage written in demonic scripture for the ritual.

"ASAS! LYSSA, BASSLY!"

From the well a monster emerged, a girl sewn by the waist onto a demon with hundreds of legs. "M-Momma…" it whispered.

"You'll serve Lord Józëne well, my child."

Scott McGregor

Scott McGregor is a Canadian writer based in Calgary, whose fiction has appeared in several anthologies by Nocturnal Sirens, Hellbound Books, DBND Publishing, Thurston Howl, and many others. He is also a student at Mount Royal University, currently finishing up his last year of English studies. His honours project explored Marxism in literature. Board games, movies, and Xbox achievement hunting are some of his other passions. You can reach him at www.scottmcgregorwrites.com or on Twitter @ScottMSays.

A Price for Death
Amber M. Simpson

The coins clinked in Selda's pocket as she ducked into the pub—payment for her latest request. Though she preferred sticking to simple moon spells and potions, the price promised for this job had been too high to ignore.

She waited for her target to go to the bathroom, then Selda rushed in behind to wrap her fingers around the woman's throat. The woman instantly changed. Her hair turned white, her skin sagging and graying as her body withered into a dried-up corpse.

Selda snuck from the pub and escaped unseen into the night, the coins jingling merrily in her pocket.

Amber M. Simpson

Amber M. Simpson writes from Northern Kentucky, with a particular interest in horror and dark fantasy. Her work has been published (both fiction and poetry) in multiple anthologies, in magazines, and online. She assists with editing for Fantasia Divinity Magazine & Publishing, where she has gotten to work with many talented authors from all over the world.

While she loves to create dark worlds and diverse characters, her greatest creations of all are her sons, Maxamus and Liam, who keep her feet on the ground even while her head is in the clouds.

Find her online at: https://www.ambermsimpson.com

Damballa
Lamont A. Turner

In her dreams Damballa appeared as a great, white serpent. He slithered between her legs and she rode him to the house of the houngan, who had made her father a zombie. Finding her father she poured salt into his mouth, breaking the spell upon him. Taking his hand she led him to his grave.

With the sunrise came the beat of drums, signaling the demise of a man of prominence. She walked to the town square where she learned of the death of Papa Duvalier, a local doctor. He had been strangled.

The houngan was dead.

Damballa is just.

Jack O' Lantern
Lamont A. Turner

He scooped out her brains with his silver ladle and flung them into the bucket. Nasty things, brains. They always left a smelly residue that clung to the sides of the cranium no matter how much he scraped. He dug out the eyes and clipped off the nose, a chain through the ears serving as a handle.

At last she was ready.

Roaming the cemetery with his new lantern he handed out treats from his brain bucket to the hungry dead rushing up to greet him. It was Halloween, a time to reward the spirits and demons who served him.

Last Words
Lamont A. Turner

"I ain't scared!" The young man shouted, his grip tightening on the shotgun.

"Then how come you ain't fired yet?" the older man taunted.

"I just don't think it's right ta kill a man who ain't hadda chance ta make his peace with the Lord."

The man under the hood mumbled in agreement.

"Alright," said the older man, yanking the hood away and peeling the tape off the man's mouth. "Pray."

Already on his knees, the man whispered something incomprehensible. The wind howled. A second later he was watching them burn. His prayer had been answered; his gods acted fast.

The Apple Thief
Lamont A. Turner

He scraped the maggots from his steak and pinned it down with his fork. As he sliced the meat oozed black bile. He couldn't do it! No matter how hungry, he couldn't make himself eat it! The repulsiveness of his food had increased, along with his hunger, since they'd dared him to climb the wall surrounding the warlock's abode. He had accepted, bringing back an apple from the warlock's orchard as proof.

The apple had bled when he bit into it, just like his arm was doing now. He finally found something he could eat.

Last Statement Of A Grave Robber
Lamont A. Turner

I was first to defile the burial chamber, yet I would be last to receive vengeance. As I pen this final testament I can see the shadow of a thing with the head of a jackal on the wall of my study. Suddenly, I know my fate. I wouldn't die like Clark, crushed beneath a statue of the pharaoh, nor would I share the fate of Nigel, blinded by the claws of a favorite pet. My body shall replace those stolen bones. Guided by the magic of the ancient dead, Anubis has come to drag me back to the tomb.

Lamont A. Turner

Lamont Turner is a New Orleans area writer whose work has appeared in numerous print and online venues.

A Stroll Down Memory Lane
Alex Azar

Ophelia remembers the warning ominously whispered to her when she found the handheld mirror in the river. The elderly widow saw her reflection not as she is, but as she was years prior. The mirror of memories most treasured returns her to happiness long past.

Before the stillbirth Ophelia sees the positive pregnancy test, a smile forming.

Further back she revisits her Parisian vacation, eyes watering.

Earlier still her wedding night sends the tears flowing.

Memories replay for days while her rictus grows permanent, eyes running dry. Her body starves and rots. Ophelia's heart beats one final time, blissfully unaware.

Alex Azar

Born and raised in New Jersey, Alex Azar is an author working primarily in the horror and mystery genres. Alex was first published in 2010 and has since published over a dozen short stories, including his award winning collection "Nightmare Noir." He is a two time winner of the Preditors & Editors Best Horror Short Story of the year award. Still in Jersey, Alex lives with his wife and their instruments of death, better known as cats, Leonidas and Miles.

Azarrising.com

Zombieland Walden
Henry Herz (with apologies to Henry David Thoreau)

I studied the dark art of necromancy to survive deliberately, and to follow the thirty rules of zombie slaying. I did not wish, when I must die, to discover that I had not lived. I did not cower at Walden Pond, nor did I wish to practice resignation to the apocalypse. I wanted to forage widely and suck the cream filling from Twinkies, to live so sturdily and Spartan-like as to put to rout all that was undead, to cut a broad swath through zombie swarms with my H2, to drive them into a corner and reduce them to pulp.

Henry Herz

Henry Herz has authored over 25 traditionally published short stories, including eight for SFWA-qualifying markets. He's authored 11 traditionally published books for children. Henry is co-editing two upcoming anthologies: THE HITHERTO SECRET EXPERIMENTS OF MARIE CURIE (Blackstone Publishing) and COMING OF AGE (Albert Whitman & Co.)

His website is www.henryherz.com

Sightless
Derek Dunn

Aunt Tabitha had quite the collection of antiques and unusual trinkets in her house. She was an eccentric woman with a flair for the supernatural.

"What are these?" said Kevin. He lifted two stones from the kitchen table.

Paul snatched them from his friend. "I think my aunt uses these to see the future?"

"No way! How do they work?"

"I don't know." Paul raised the smooth stones to his eyes. He peered into their glassy surfaces, and then shrieked in pain. As he pulled his hands from his face Kevin saw only the charred remains of his friend's eyes.

True Love's Last Kiss
Derek Dunn

Sir Aleyn climbed the final steps of the castle's tallest tower. He smiled upon seeing the princess. Her lifeless body lay on the bed, covered by a black veil.

The knight pulled back the cloth from her face and touched his lips to hers. A searing pain stung his side. He dropped to his knees, blood seeped through his tunic. The princess rose from the bed, a bloodied knife in hand. She struck again, sending Sir Aleyn to the floor.

He looked up at the woman. Fire burned in her evil eyes. This wasn't the princess he'd meant to awaken.

Derek Dunn

Derek Dunn is an author of dark fiction whose works have appeared in anthologies by Black Hare Press, Blood Song Books, Reanimated Writers Press, and Eerie River Publishing. He's been a musician and film enthusiast for many years and received a bachelor's degree in Media Arts Studies. Derek lives in the American northwest with his family, dog, and fish.

Disappearance to the Dark Realm
John Cady

With a stage name like the 'Amazing Antonio' I thought he'd be anything but. So, when he invited me to step into his vanishing chest, I expected the back to open for me to roll on out and disappear offstage. Instead, I disappeared into the Dark Realm.

The air there was heavy, suffocating me where I stood. The shadows surrounding me took on human form, but there were no bodies from which they were cast. Wails echoed against nearby walls and were soon joined by my own. Panic had indeed set in; I could see no escape from this madness.

John Cady

John Cady was born and raised in Massachusetts. Upon graduating from Manhattan College, he returned to his hometown to begin his teaching career. When he isn't teaching the English Language Arts to incarcerated youth, he is writing.

Kulilu
Holley Cornetto

She reached out with webbed hands and fingers like talons. She pulled me close, sinking her teeth deep into my flesh. The pain pulsed, then dulled. When she pulled away I saw my skin and flesh between her teeth. Suddenly the air around me was oppressive, and I felt like I was drowning. The world grew darker, smaller, and then all around me was blackness.

I opened my eyes and found myself beneath the ocean's surface. I touched the gashes on my neck – gills where the bite marks had been.

"Welcome, beloved." Her voice was as cold as the sea.

Poppet
Holley Cornetto

I travelled the forest path to the ring of ancient trees that had somehow grown in a perfect circle. I approached the large stone altar in the center. On it lay poppets strung together from sticks and rotting leaves.

Take one.

Had I heard it, or thought it?

I lifted the smallest one, the one that wore the same dress as my baby sister. Beside it there was a mistletoe stake.

I buried the stake in the doll's chest.

When I returned home I would place the changeling's poppet in my sister's cradle, then they would come to collect her.

Holley Cornetto

Holley Cornetto was born and raised in Alabama, but now lives in New Jersey. To indulge her love of books and stories, she became a librarian. She is also a writer, because the only thing better than being surrounded by stories is to create them herself. She can be found lurking on Twitter @HLCornetto.

Eye on the Prize
J.W. Garrett

The portal opened, saving Eric from the inhuman creature tailing him. Where was he? Lifting his head he stepped into the unknown world, shuddering from his narrow escape. He clutched at the treasure, protected by dark magic from a blood sacrifice.

Shadows blocked sunlight, the familiar sweep of heavy wings cutting the air. The dragon swooped low, drawn by the jewel. Fire licked Eric's heels as he murmured a spell, disappearing from sight.

The dragon chomped hard, freeing the bubble from invisible bindings. The jewel pulsed red, boring into the animal's eyes. Unfettered, the demon transformed and soared for home.

Life's Toil
J.W. Garrett

The gathered hovered among their prey, waiting before the army paraded forward, ending life in its path. The wraith's jaw yawned open, methodically consuming one soul in a slow crawl of death before taking the next victim. There was no hurry, nowhere else to run. With all the supply of souls before them converted to fuel, the war would be over soon enough.

The wraith paused, captivated at a human's struggle to maintain his pitiful existence. Why, when they would now power the universe? The struggle done a silver weapon glimmered from the remains, its magic impotent where it lay.

J.W. Garrett

J.W. Garrett is a multi-award-winning author. Initiated into fantasy after reading The Hobbit in elementary school, she has been hooked ever since. She writes speculative fiction from the sunny beaches of Jacksonville, Florida, but loves the mountains of Virginia where she was born. Her writings include novels, short stories, and poetry. Since completing Remeon's Crusade, the third book in her sci-fi fantasy series, Realms of Chaos, she has been hard at work on the next installment. When she's not hanging out with her characters, her favorite activities are reading, running and spending time with family.

Website: www.jwgarrett.com
BHC Press: www.bhcpress.com/Author_JW_Garrett.html

The Hanged Woman
Lucy Rose

The people from the hamlet know to stay well away from the wood, for fear of disappearing. The forest was decaying from the inside out, and at the source of rot a woman hung from the branch of an ancient tree.

Her feet swung, limp and grey. Blackened toenails fastened skin to bone. Her face, which had grown weary of human qualities, harboured no feeling. Ants had tunnelled through her bone marrow and found their way up her spine, crawling out from her face in neat lines.

The hanged woman began to speak. She told me I, too, would disappear.

Lucy Rose

Lucy Rose (INFP/T) is a prose writer and an award-winning writer/director. Her most recent film, 'She Lives Alone', was financed by the BFI Network and is currently visiting festivals, a number of which are BAFTA & Oscar-qualifying. Words for Small Leaf Press, Boshemia, SINK Magazine, The Selkie, Kandisha Press and more. @lucyrosecreates

Celebration
Emma K. Leadley

The faeries danced round the fire. Sparks of flame shot into the night sky and firebugs swarmed. The portal to Earth shimmered, then finally vanished forever.

"To the last of the humans," shouted a faery, their wings sparkling brightly, their hair purple in the glow of stars, moonlight and blazing celebration.

"To the last," the others replied, crunching on bones and ripping raw sinews apart with their sharp teeth. As they gorged their wings shone brighter, their laughter becoming more raucous.

They tossed fatty tissue and tough skin into the fire until singed flesh and fatty smoke filled the air.

Hell Broth
Emma K. Leadley

"Eye of newt, toe of frog, wool of bat, tongue of dog," the witch intoned, bored. Making a Hell-broth was beginner stuff. Why they had to successfully repeat it so many times to enter the academy was beyond their comprehension.

"Adder's fork, blindworm's sting, lizard's leg, and -— *fuck!* – what is it?"

The cauldron boiled and bubbled, a dark shadow rising from within. It solidified, becoming a monstrous, fleshy mishmash of everything the cauldron contained, and it was hungry for blood.

The witch screamed as it ripped them apart. Watching, the academy board shook their heads.

Another potential candidate lost.

Emma K. Leadley

Emma K. Leadley, (she/they) is a UK-based writer, creative geek, and devourer of words, images and ideas. She began writing both fiction and creative non-fiction as an outlet for her busy brain, and quickly realised scrawling words on a page is wired into her DNA. Visit her online at https://emmaleadley.co.uk or on Twitter @autoerraticism.

The Forbidden Arts
Dale Parnell

"Apprentice Page, you stand accused of meddling in the forbidden arts. Do you have anything you wish to say to the Masters here assembled?"

The Chamber of Judgement was a rotting, vainglorious room full of decrepit, jealous fools.

"I have not meddled," the man once called Apprentice said, "I have conquered."

The chamber hummed and sparked as the Old Words were spoken, and one by one the Masters fell dead; helpless, wide-eyed, silent.

"The sacrifice is accepted," came a voice older than time and memory, colder than death itself. "What would you have us show you?"

"Everything," whispered Master Page.

The Final War
Dale Parnell

"The Fae are all cowards," the guard exclaimed, spittle flecking his lips, "hiding behind tricks and glamours. You must always be on watch, young lad."

"That you must," the lad replied, burying his sword into the guard's exposed back. With gloved hands he retrieved the iron key, easing open the door of the warded cell. "It is time, Your Majesty," the lad said, his true form shimming into being.

"And my army?" the King asked.

"The Distant Lands lay empty, Majesty. We stand as one. What are your orders?"

"The humans must learn," the King said firmly. "Kill them all."

Fire and Madness
Dale Parnell

Ours is the last human outpost; a final, hopeless stand against impossible creatures older than the mountains. As the sun slowly fades the tempest builds once again, each gust born on a wingbeat.

They break through our defences as if they were paper and straw, teeth stained red with the blood of all those who fell before us. They bring with them fire and madness. Driven blind with terror we turn on each other, axes hacking away limbs and splitting skulls. In truth it is less painful to die by our own hands than to beg mercy from a dragon.

DALE PARNELL

Dale Parnell lives in Staffordshire, England, with his wife and their imaginary dog, Moriarty. He writes short fiction, mainly fantasy, science-fiction and horror, along with the occasional poem. He has self-published two collections of short stories, along with a poetry collection to date, and is lucky enough to feature in a number of excellent fiction and poetry anthologies.

You can find Dale on Facebook at www.facebook.com/shortfictionauthor
Instagram at www.instagram.com/shortfictionauthor

The Witch's Tree
Josh Grant-Young

There is a forest where a sole tree stands: bent, weathered, nearly split by lightning and rife with charcoal. The 'Witch's Tree', the locals call it, resides deep within the sunless reaches of the wood. Black carvings and occult sigils cut deep into the barkless trunk.

Here I unpack my tools to make another mark. My aim is to call forth, as others have, the spirits deep within the soil whose souls are contorted like the roots which hold them imprisoned. I whisper incantations as I make my first cut, heeding the wailing of the wind. It cries in anger.

Josh Grant-Young

Josh Grant-Young is a doctoral candidate at the University of Guelph, where he studies horror film. In his spare time, he enjoys watching, reading, and writing horror.

Twitter: @jgrantyoung1

It's Not
Georgia Cook

White-haired they found him — white-haired and delirious on the edge of the forest, blood on his clothes and madness in his eyes.

"It's Not - !" he gasped, as he died in their arms. *"It's Not - !"*

They never found the girl — his beautiful, young wife — and all assumed him a murderer. But they found the child, with its smiling mouth and wide, yellow eyes, snuggled safe between the roots of an oak tree. And none were particularly surprised when it too vanished from its crib on the next full moon, nor did any go to search for it.

It's Not - ! It's Not - !

Down In The Deep Dark
Georgia Cook

Deep below the earth the Dwarves toiled, without lamps and without maps, for guidance. Through echoing caverns and buried temples they whispered prayers to gods nobody above ground had heard for millenias -- gods of airlessness and tight gaps, gods of fresh seams and glittering gemstones, Gods of the Crush and the Choke.

Keep us safe.
Keep our footing sure.
Guide us.

Not dragons they feared -- not sudden jets of flame, nor the whispers of the dead -- but the soft rumbling, heard down in the deepest dark in tunnels no dwarf dared venture. Something vast grew, something unstoppable climbing ever upwards.

Faerie Fruit
Georgia Cook

They'd warned her never to accept food offered by the fae -- not their fruits, not their wine, not their pretty, little morsels -- or else she would be lost to them. She'd be kept with the faeries in their chasms deep below the earth, far from the world above.

No more home, or farm. No more marriage to a man who saw her as nothing so much as his prize. No more of the life she had lived for fifteen years.

And as she laughed, drinking deep from her second goblet, she knew that this was the sweetest promise of all.

And The Prince Gave Chase
Georgia Cook

Tearstained and sobbing she stumbled through the forest, briars stinging her arms and tearing her dress, branches tangling in her rich, black hair.

Alone. Alone. *Utterly* alone. No magic now, no fairy godmother, no bold knight to rescue her.

The ballgown glistened, even in total darkness -- glistened like jewels, glistened like a ghost, like the promise of a prince enraged to find himself deceived that she was no princess after all.

At her back, off between the trees, a howl went up, followed by another and another. The pounding of hooves. The cry of the hunt.

Not alone after all.

Georgia Cook

Georgia Cook is an illustrator and writer from London, specialising in folklore and ghost stories. She is the winner of the LISP 2020 Flash Fiction Prize, and has been shortlisted for the Bridport Prize, Staunch Book Prize and Reflex Fiction Award, among others. She can be found on twitter at @georgiacooked and on her website at https://www.georgiacookwriter.com/

Ash and Wing
S.N. Graves

Harold would love her forever.

His heart was bound in blood—the wound on her palm fresh from the atheme. A little songbird wrapped in tissue twitched once again, the darning needle piercing its breast clicking frantically against the marble countertop. She lit a match and let the bundle of bird, blood and small remembrances of Harold burn—a bit of his hair, a note he'd slipped to Suzy in the hall.

Do you like me?

Check the box. Yes or no?

Forget about it, Suzy. Ash and bird blazed away; he was hers now.

Harold would love her forever.

S.N. Graves

S.N. Graves earned her MFA in Popular Fiction from Seton Hill University in 2014 and was a senior editor at Loose Id LLC until it closed its doors. She is now a professor at Southern New Hampshire University, teaching genre fiction with a concentration in horror. Graves also freelance edits and creates art, including book covers.

Website: www.sngraves.com

The Queen's Debt
Marsha Webb

Darkness enveloped the swamp. The sludgy layer rippled, emitting a gloppy echo.

A red horn emerged, quickly followed by the head, wings and body of the Skeeter Imp. Its harrowing cry alerted the rest of the pack. They circled, squawking deafeningly.

Today was the promised day they overthrew the queen, and the Underworld became theirs.

"Fetch the queen," chanted the skeeters until the queen was brought before them. "Leave our realm."

"Please, no," she begged, but the debt needed to be paid. She was forced deep into the swamp until silver swirls rose into the air.

Marsha Webb

Marsha Webb is a teacher in a high school in Cardiff. She have been writing for the last few years and had a number of short stories and poetry published in themed anthologies and online sites and magazines.

Her first novel "You can choose your sin but you cannot choose the consequences" was published last year and has received good reviews.

The Last Dragon's Sacrifice
Lyndsey Ellis-Holloway

How long had it been since the others had given their lives?

He couldn't recall.

A millennium was a long time to be alone, even for a dragon.

The humans had grown bold, their selfish acts destroying the Earth around them.

He watched and waited, hoping they would learn… but they didn't.

At Everest's peak he let the cold seep into his very soul. His body turned to stone, merging with the mountain. He would give his life to maintain the barrier separating the humans and the magical world, and prayed it would last long enough for humans to change.

The Halfing-Child's Revenge
Lyndsey Ellis-Holloway

Beaten. Bloodied. Bruised.

Every day the same torment, every moment filled with agony because they hated her existence. How could *she* be held accountable for who her mother lay with?

She suffered the consequences of it nonetheless.

No matter.

She'd met her father now, brief though their tryst was, and he had shown her *exactly* what she was.

She giggled, dancing through the burning city.

Her flames, released from their prison within her heart, embraced the girl as they took vengeance on those that had wronged her.

They couldn't hurt her anymore – now it was *her* turn to torment *them*.

The Archangel of Grief
Lyndsey Ellis-Holloway

The Archangel of Grief had done her duty with relish.

Answering the mournful cries of Heaven, Hell and Earth alike – devouring the Grief of every living being. She bore the weight of all that pain, alone.

She never hesitated to save another from drowning in their Sorrow.

Artiya'il watched as Heaven marched upon Hell and Earth, intent on destruction.

Storm-grey eyes turned black as she called forth the Grief of millennia.

The misery she had collected flowed from her body, standing behind her as shadowy figures, an army of pure Despair.

Time for Grief to go to war with Heaven.

Curse of the Nekomata
Lyndsey Ellis-Holloway "Here kitty!"

The cat wiggled his two tails, smiling as the boy followed him.

Deeper, deeper into the forest they went, the light swallowed by the trees.

As the cat disappeared into the darkness the boy whimpered.

"Kitty?"

Standing on it's back legs it loomed over the boy, giving a malevolent smile as it gathered him into its arms.

"I'm right here. We all are," it said wickedly.

The forest filled with a hundred pairs of blood-red eyes.

Ignoring the panicked cries of the villagers the Nekomata stole the boy away into the night, twin tails setting the forest alight.

I am The Kolm
Lyndsey Ellis-Holloway

His attack collided with my chest, the magic tingled against my stone skin.

Tilting my head to one side I smiled at the Wizard. Did he really think that pathetic little incantation would stop me?

I could see the fear in his eyes, the color draining from his face.

He had underestimated Master's need for revenge, misjudged Master's ability.

I was here to hunt him and the other Wizards who wronged my Master.

They would pay.

The Wizard whimpered as I stepped toward him, claws bared.

No magic can harm me, and my bloodthirst is unparalleled.

I am The Kolm.

Lyndsey Ellis-Holloway

Lyndsey Ellis-Holloway is a writer from Knaresborough, UK. She writes fantasy, sci-fi, horror and dystopian stories, focussing on compelling characters and layering in myth and legend at every opportunity.

Her mind is somewhat dark and twisted, and she lives in perpetual hope of owning her own Dragon someday, but for now she writes about them to fill the void… and to stop her from murdering people who annoy her.

When she's not writing she spends time with her husband, her dogs and her friends enjoying activities such as walking, movies, conventions and of course writing for fun as well!

https://theprose.com/LyndseyEH
Twitter: @LEllisHolloway

Currents
Sonya Lawson

The river was flooding at an unnatural rate, but she didn't notice. She was focused on her smiling mother who waded in the waters along the reedy bank, waving for her to come closer. She laughed with delight as she reached a hand forward, noticing too late the hoof that emerged when the creature stepped up to tightly grip her. A memory hit, hard. Her mother's funeral had been just two weeks ago, but the realization came too late. The kelpie dove into the rising waters, quickly dragging her out past the currents before she could even cry for help.

Bauble
Sonya Lawson

"I'm sorry," John sighed, gently stroking her bruised cheek. Mary nodded and whispered, "I know," while tears slid down her face. "But look at this pretty bauble I made for you." He dangled a white crystal on a black, leather band from his hand. It glowed softly from within. "Put it on." Mary slipped it over her head, the jagged stone feeling like a heavy weight when it thudded between her breasts. It glowed more brightly, then began to pulse, picking up the same rhythm as her heart. She became like stone herself, mind blank and ready for his command.

A Real Page-Turner
Sonya Lawson

The book opened on its own, flipping back and forth quickly until it stilled on a page. Circe peered down, muttering to herself, "Of course, the Ándras Gouroúni hex. So simple. Why did I not think of that?" She smiled and hummed as she scanned the page to refresh her memory. Above her a man whimpered in a rusted, iron cage. She reached up to pat his dangling leg. He flinched, but Circe just chuckled. "This will all be over soon, lovey," she cooed up at him. "I haven't used this hex in millennia, but it worked just fine then."

Sonya Lawson

Sonya Lawson is a recovering academic. She has published several nonfiction works in academic journals and essay collections but is now working on more speculative fiction. While she will always be a rural Kentuckian at heart, she currently lives in the Pacific Northwest. Her days are filled with writing, editing, reading, walking old forests, and watching sitcoms or horror films with her partner and their cat. You can follow her occasional ramblings on Twitter (@Sonyawazhere).

The Date
Spencer Helsel

"How's your steak, sweetie? Tastes good?" She raised her wine glass to her lips. "I want everything to be perfect for you. I love you."

"I love you, too."

Did I? Something was wrong. I looked down; the steak and greens were rotten. Maggots crawled from the steak's flesh and slimy vegetables over my hands—

—my hands that lay immobile on either side of the plate. Maggots crawled between my rotting fingers.

"You cheated on me," she said, "but killing you wasn't enough, sweetie. I brought you back, now we can be together. Forever."

I tried to scream.

I couldn't.

The Tutor
Spencer Helsel

"It's pronounced with a soft 'G'," Mark told her, sitting across the library table from her, "like 'gentle.'"

Claire tried again.

He shook his head, she groaned.

"You'll get it. Pronunciation is difficult. Everyone struggles at first."

"But you said pronunciation is everything, otherwise no one understands me," she griped.

"Yes, but you have to remember: it's a different language, and a dead one at that. Try again."

She cussed loudly.

"Shh!" He chided. "Volume! It's a library!"

"Who cares?"

He shrugged. "True. Try again."

She did.

Floating above them the librarian writhed in agony.

Mark grinned. "Perfect! Once more."

Spencer Helsel

Spencer Helsel was born in Culpeper, Virginia. He earned his Bachelor's Degree from Christopher Newport University and has spent the last decade as a middle school and high school teacher.

He currently lives with his wife and three sons wherever the military sends them.

Lenten Lament of the Rougarou
Nick Wilkinson

Adolpha danced among the ominous Cypress trees, a crescent moon hanging low over the pestilential swamp. She never broke her Lenten promises on purpose; she was content worshiping among the choir of frogs and mosquitoes, croaking and buzzing primordial hymns.

She was deep in prayer, feverish from the holy heat of her personal Vigil Mass. Adolpha heard a series of howls and huffs through the humidity and harmony; they were too close for comfort. Startled, she turned with caution. She now found herself surrounded. She locked eyes with a feral pack of blood-soaked, ravenous wolf-like Rougarou.

The family was home.

En-Naddāha
Nick Wilkinson

The Nile water spread out before him, Ahmed leans back in silent contemplation. No longer alone, a soft sleepy song calls out; a series of intoxicating vocalizations gliding over the great river. Harmonic and terrifying the song of the Naiads entrance Ahmed, an enchanted incantation pulling him toward the ancient, mystifying waters.

It was as if the maidens of the deep lassoed his soul, beckoning their would-be lover to come and get devoured. Wavering at the water's edge he descends. Delicate hands claw away, stealing the last of his heat. A blood-soaked Ahmed sinks, surrendering his body and soul.

NICK WILKINSON

Nick Wilkinson is a writer from Philadelphia, PA now living in Kearny, AZ. In his spare time he likes to spend time with his wife and daughters, as well as spin tales and poems for the world to read.

Summoning a Demon
Neen Cohen

Blood dripped from the knife. His forearm burned as beads of blood rose, darkening the star carved into his flesh.

"Come, servant of blood, demon of my bloodline."

"Servant?" The voice brought images of gravel crushed beneath machinery. The demon rose, making the man's 6 foot height look as though he were a child.

"I demand you bow to me." His voice wavered and the demon smiled, viscus dripping from his fangs and bloody lips.

"Humans."

The demon's laughter loosened the man's bowels moments before he saw the demon's talons release his entrails to the floor before him.

"Kill me."

They Beg for Mercy
Neen Cohen

Blood glistens on the black hoofs as they slow to a walk. On top of the beast is a woman who glows bright-white, save for the smears of blood that decorate her skin and regal dress.

"When are they going to learn to stop calling on us?" A man guides his own blood-spattered beast beside her mount.

"Never, I hope." She throws back her head and her laughter thunders through the sky, lightning trailing behind it.

They step past the broken bodies of humans who begged for mercy. Magic was never designed to protect the weak, and nor were angels.

What Mercy Death Would Be
Neen Cohen

His body shivers against the cold, wrists raw and bleeding from the ropes.

"Ar-are you vampires?" He pushed the question out between cracked, dry lips.

"Oh, sweety," She jams the end of the metal straw back into his neck and takes a deep drink of his warm, rich blood. "We're the thing the vampires hide from."

On the couch a second woman lays, her mouth stained with his lifeforce. Her laughter makes him sob uncontrollably.

"Kill me, please..."

"No."

She flicks her wrist, and his body begins to replenish itself. Each drop of blood is acid on nerves.

He screams.

Fairy Lights
Neen Cohen

The beauty of her face was hidden behind scars and a scowl. Her wings, likewise damaged, flapped slowly.

I reached out my hand to stroke her cheek.

The scowl deepened, her mouth opening wider than any jaw should allow.

"Arrrgggghhhh!" I tried to pull my finger away from her clamped teeth, shaking my hand fiercely, but she hung on until my screaming stopped.

I followed, one footstep and then another, before collapsing to the ground.

My veins spread black beneath my skin.

The lights surround me.

I had found the fairy kingdom.

How long until my body would be found?

Neen Cohen

Neen Cohen is an LGBTQI and speculative fiction author. Her short stories and drabbles can be found in anthologies through several different publishers. She is a member of the Springfield Writers Group.

Neen lives in Brisbane Australia with her partner, son, and fur babies. She loves to roam cemeteries, botanic gardens, and construction sites and can often be found writing while sitting against a tree or tombstone.

Check out her latest adventures at https://linktr.ee/neencohen

Wielding the Unexpected
Matthew Tansek

Hendrix caught the spell on the wind and sent it spiraling back impotently.

Then, shedding energy like a dog shaking off water, he repulsed the next salvo against him. The elements were too predictable, and his mind veered off into the weeds searching for the unexpected.

His nightmares came back to him, and he remembered. He had communed with the worms that eat worlds, and felt the gnawing aether that drifts behind time. In slumber he had wandered the slime hells, and bellowed with the audient darkness.

He smiled at his new arsenal; he now would have the upper hand.

Wrath of Ice
Matthew Tansek

The great pyre had been satiated, the litany had been chanted and the three wisest had gone to the peak of the sentinel hill to commune with the divine.

Yet still the wrath was coming.

Like an impenetrable dread palisade the storm clouds advanced, flickering with anger. Those that knew the old stories did not bother to board the doors, or shelter themselves in cover, for it was said that those that betrayed the gods would be entombed in ice.

The blasphemous magics had halted the great glacier, but the sky could not be warded against.

They were doomed.

Cheques and balances
K.T. Tate

Everything has a price. I wanted love - it was tragic how my ex died, but you were more than happy to comfort me. We needed money - your parents were old, and very generous in their will. You wanted that promotion - your boss' heart attack was a welcome shock.

You never suspected the blood I'd spilt, the pacts I'd made to give us this perfect life. Even for your unborn child your sister lost hers, and now I catch you fucking the neighbour!

Through angry tears I draw the unholy sigils, penning your name.

Let's find out what you are worth.

Fountain of Youth
K.T. Tate

He grins excitedly as I push him onto the bed. The silk scarf elicits a moan as I bind him, the blindfold hiding my sins as I trace symbols on him in wax and scratches. He devours every sensual punishment as I weave my spell.

Repeatedly I bring him to the edge, until he is begging for release.

"Say you're mine, body and soul."

"I'm yours…body and soul," He whimpers as I lower myself onto him.

Gasping, the symbols alight. I take more than his seed into me. My body renews as his screams echo. Oh, the price of immortality.

Tree of Knowledge
K.T. Tate

It burns my eyes, but I can't stop. Words I shouldn't understand evaporate from the grimoire's page. Sneaking through the now-bloody canals of my ears towards my brain, unholy secrets stack like razors in my mind.

I can't let go of the book. The cover's eldritch symbols creep onto my skin, settling like nesting spiders and burrowing into my flesh. Scarred into place, making me a tapestry of the occult.

My head pounds with forbidden knowledge. *Things* from beyond push at me, barely kept at bay. My sight fades as the final words fill me. Blinded, I now see everything.

Flesh of My Flesh
K.T. Tate

A cry echoes from my sister's room. I hear our parents rushing to her side as I stick the pin further into my flesh. I twist it back and forth, fuelled by my hatred.

Blood pours.

I was smart. I was meant to enchant a doll, but who better to represent my twin than me? Now she will literally feel all my pain.

I pull out more pins and sink them under my fingernails; her screams of agony are like a symphony to me. I raise a pin to my eye. Brady won't like her so much when she's blind.

Forbidden Fruit
K.T. Tate

I shouldn't have stolen from that witch's orchard. We didn't need the fruit, but I wanted it so badly. I couldn't resist trying the apple on the way home.

Delicious.

The shotgun blast doesn't stop me as I shamble towards my wife. She smells like cinnamon apple pie. She's pleading, but I'm so hungry. Her sweet scent fills my nostrils. I indulge, tearing at her succulent flesh. Crying with sorrow and delight I chew, swallowing greedily. She's the best thing I've ever tasted.

Then a new scent peaks my senses, something even more tempting. I turn to see my children.

K.T. Tate

K.T. Tate is an English author inspired to write speculative fiction. She draws on her love of horror to explore the themes of cosmic and occult horror, the supernatural, folktales and witchcraft. Writing mainly drabbles and short stories, her works have been featured in a plethora of anthologies. All of which can be found on her website below.

Website – www.eldritch-hollow.com

The Cost
L. T. Emery

All magic has a cost.

My teacher never told me. Until, on his deathbed, my ancient mentor revealed the price of every spell I cast.

One spell.

One death.

The death of an innocent mother or father, brother or sister. The death of a newborn baby.

I was livid. All the times I used a smidgen of magic to breathe life into a candle or turn the page of my spell-book, a death. All magic is black, I see.

The cost on my soul is too much. I have concocted a spell to bring them all back...my last spell.

The Last Witch
L. T. Emery

I watched my best friend's eyes bulge out of their sockets as she hangs. Another witch trial victim.

I'm next. I feel the accusation coming.

I cast a spell to bear a creature, made to always protect me.

The spider crawls from the smoking, stinking caldron and scuttles out my open door. Growing with monstrous speed, the arachnid balloons until it's what my colleagues in the east call a kaiju.

Horror fills me as it crushes whole houses with each step. This isn't what I intended. Everyone's dead. I have no friends now, but at least they'll never hang me.

The Battle for the Skies
L. T. Emery

Rose flew through a sky of dragons upon Horizon, her beast. The battle for the skies was scorching and bloody. Dragons of Light and Dark fell amid a cannonade of fireballs, corkscrewing to their doom.

Rose, a soldier of Light, had taken out countless Dark warriors, but while soldiers of Light waned warriors of Dark seemed only to increase.

In a moment of distraction Horizon was hit. It was over.

"I don't want to die!" Rose screamed, falling.

"Join ussss." A voice hissed.

Without thought Rose agreed. Black magic fizzed, stealing her soul, and another Dark warrior entered the fray.

DIY Black Magic
L. T. Emery

'Do-it-yourself Black Magic' read the box.

A sleepover imminent, my best friend and I clubbed our money together and bought the game, our entertainment for the night.

The spells were numerous, from brewing love potions to talking to the dead, but the one that took our fancy was a binding.

"We're best friends," I said, "let's make sure we'll always be together."

Pricking our fingers we mingled our blood and chanted the incantation.

The screaming began as the spell took hold. The pain was excruciating, half our bodies melting into nothingness before zipping together; one lopsided, mismatched horror...together forever.

Recession
L. T. Emery

Demons scuttle and soar throughout the city, massacring all. Homes fall, supermarkets burn and pets explode like popcorn kernels.

The smell of burning flesh ignites my hunger, a hunger so deep and clawing my very soul longs for sustenance.

In these times of flying cars and artificial intelligence there is little work for witches like me. I salivate, knowing those left when I close the gates of Hell will need me again. They'll sell me little bits of their souls to get spells for food and protection.

Business is about to boom, and my hunger will be a distant memory.

L. T. Emery

L. T. Emery is a British author, with a love for Horror, Sci-fi and Fantasy genres.

He is the proud father of one and husband to the love of his life. Outside of family life, he is an avid reader of novels, genre magazines, comics, manga and just about anything else he can get his hands on. With a particular love of long form fiction, he is currently working on a fantasy novel which he hopes to publish in the future. He can be found online at https://ltemery.wixsite.com/homeand and twitter.com/ltemeryuk

You can find his works in Black Hare Press, Eerie River and Macabre Ladies anthologies.

To Feel More Alive
Kaitlyn Arnett

It was addicting, the thrill of magic racing through his veins. *Nothing* compared to the rush of adrenaline that came with each use of his power, and Adriam doubted anything ever would.

The power he'd been born with was nothing, unstable and useless.

But this?

This was absolutely *exhilarating.*

He turned to face his silent observer, a cold smile on blood-stained lips. "Thank you, darling," he said. "Your gift will be appreciated, of course."

They didn't answer, their soul departed and body hollow.

Adriam laughed. If this brilliant *rush* was the reward for death, then he'd take it without hesitation.

KAITLYN ARNETT

Kaitlyn Arnett is a teen author from Temecula, California. She primarily writes drabbles and short stories, usually in the fantasy and sci-fi genres.

The Bard's Arrow
Kris Kinsella

The Cutpurse presses the edge of the dagger to his surprised victim's throat before whispering a stern threat into his ear.

The Bard crinkles his face at the thief's stench, before replying with a low, sweet melody. The eons-old song dances in the air before worming its way into the Cutpurse's ears, where it pierces deep within the man's soul.

The dagger falls to the cobblestone with a clatter as the Bard walks away, whistling cheerfully. The Cutpurse collapses to the ground, tears streaking his face, as the Bard's spell curses him with the poison of empathy for his victims!

The Fall of Pompei
Kris Kinsella

Thick drops of acrid crimson fall onto the battlefield, scorching the earth and sizzling the skin of the soldiers beneath the hazy fog of war.

Hope grows, spreading from man to man, thick spears heavy in their hands. *Could it really be over?* The eyes of each man, with faces covered in dirt and blood, plead desperately.

A guttural roar from above dashes their hopes, and the weary men tighten the grasp on their spears, searching their souls for more courage.

For the God of Blood and Ash is merely wounded, not dead, and his assault on the city continues!

A Crown's Weight
Kris Kinsella

Deep in the bowels of the castle the Queen opens a door unknown to her. In the torchlight a chained creature looks up towards her with pleading eyes.

"Please…" The Muse begs, her voice euphoric in the Queen's ears despite her sordid condition. Her pale skin glows like moonlight in the darkness, and the Queen trembles with the urge to caress the Muse.

The Queen hesitates, thinking of the many years of prosperity under the good King, before closing the door on the whimpering Muse. The Queen feeling, for the first time, the true weight of the crown she wears!

Kris Kinsella

Kris Kinsella is an emerging writer from Gettysburg, PA surrounded by far too many animals. A lifelong lover of horror fiction & film, you can find him on twitter @kinsellakristof and at kriskinsella.com

That Lady Blue
Chris Bannor

"What do they call you?"

She smiled as she took a drink of her wine. It was chilled, an extravagance in this heat-stricken city. The sands baked under foot, but the leader of the oasis demanded his luxuries.

"Lady Blue," she answered, and waited.

His eyes widened and he stood abruptly, dropping the wine and spilling its content across the fine, imported rugs. She smiled as he began to cough. His blood fell from his lips and splattered onto the carpet, mixing with the wine already lost.

She answered the question that he could not speak. "Yes, *that* Lady Blue."

The Knight
Chris Bannor

"The Knight will come," he assured his companions. Everyone knew the Knight was always at the Laughing Bard's side, and they had him staked out as bait.

He felt the blade before he heard it coming, before he realized his companions had gone quiet. "You can't kill us like that," he said through bloody lips. "What of your honor?"

"You should have asked," the Knight said. "I'm no knight, I'm the Knight Killer. I have no code but my own."

The last things the thief saw before his death were the Bard's lyre and the Knight's indulging smile, then darkness.

The Baby of the Family
Chris Bannor

The ground was wet with swallowed blood, the rocks painted as if they were the teeth of some ferocious monster.

For a moment they had been.

The Knight and Blue Lady had remained spotless, but the Red Queen was blood-soaked and the Laughing Bard was grinning with shining, red blades in hand.

She was Wicked Breeze. Fae magic ran through her veins, but the Sidhe had never welcomed her. These misfits had rescued her years ago and raised her as their own. Now their family had a purpose and a plan, and she had the power to see it done.

SAVAGERY
Chris Bannor

Blood dripped, fresh and warm, through her fingers. No one would ever question her place in this world again; not the young woman who had thought to replace her, nor the husband who thought to displace her.

The court flinched as she tossed her husband's heart into the fire. The wet flesh made the wood hiss and spark, and she watched in delight. "Were there any questions?"

The Knight at her side called out, "Hail the Red Queen!"

Some believed the legend of the Red Queen was an exaggeration. They learned too late; the stories didn't do her savagery justice.

Dead Men's Tales
Chris Bannor

The fire was still high when he joined them. They called for songs, but he waved them away. They teased the Laughing Bard, but he knew his craft and he knew the time.

When the fires died low.

When ale and exhaustion caused men's wits to be slow.

When the thought of home was more important than the dangers surrounding them.

He moved swiftly, a knife here and there, catching them so they looked drunken and slovenly instead of lifeless. When he finished he sat with his lyre to compose tonight's adventure. Few ever heard his tales, except the dead.

Chris Bannor

Chris Bannor is a speculative fiction writer who lives in Southern California. Chris learned her love of genre stories from her mother at an early age and has never veered far from that path. Her stories have been published in over two dozen anthologies and range from horror and science fiction, to fantasy, romance, and steampunk.

When not writing, Chris enjoys spending time with her family and binge watching sci-fi and fantasy shows. You can chat with Chris on Facebook @chrisbannorauthor. To keep up to date with her musings and new releases, visit www.ChrisBannor.com

Blood is the Life
Elizabeth Davis

The dead dragon's blood dripped over the shining gold. The hero knelt down, running his hands through the coins as he dropped his sword. On his knees the hero looked up from his greed into the dead eyes of the dragon. "To think," he murmured, "that we may never see your kind again." The sword smirked as the blood seeped into the metal. The fool had known little about dragon blood, of what beats in a dragon's heart. The metal stretched out, feeling itself for the first time. The sword struck as the hero looked down again, still holding gold.

Deep in the Woods
Elizabeth Davis

The cottage had grown cold, but it was still the witch's cottage; that's why she ran there. She didn't bother to fill up her pockets with breadcrumbs or rocks. She pushed open the stiff door, shivering from the cold. The lightning let her see the cottage only in eye-blinks. A black cauldron rested over the fireplace, a heavy bell hung above the door and a thick book sat open on the table. She reached forward, her fingers brushing the soft pages. A single touch and the parchment rippled, just as fire appeared and the bell chimed. The witch had returned.

Elizabeth Davis

Elizabeth Davis is a second generation writer living in Dayton, Ohio.

She lives there with her spouse and two cats - neither of which have been lost to ravenous corn mazes or sleeping serpent gods. She can be found at deadfishbooks.com when she isn't busy creating beautiful nightmares and bizarre adventures. Her work can be found in, Eerie River Publishing Patreon July 2020, Eternal Haunted Summer Summer 2020, and No Safe Distance: Stories from Isolation.

Earthbound
S.O. Green

He used the cleaver and swung hard to crack the bone. Dirty, bloody work, but necessary.

She didn't cry out, didn't even flinch. He could almost have believed she didn't feel pain, but her eyes betrayed her.

"There," he said, pulling the last scrap away. "Done."

He trailed a finger over the stumps where her wings had once been. Perhaps he would mount them on the wall to remind her. Or burn them, so that she would forget.

"No tears," he warned. "It's better this way."

Now she didn't have to choose. She could stay with him, his angel forever.

Her Eternal Reward
S.O. Green

She was a pretty, young thing, this hero. Fiery hair, blood and freckles on her cheeks. Even a sword through the stomach hadn't dampened her fire. Dead, yes, but still defiant.

Malissa sighed. "What a pity."

Such a brave warrior deserved better than to lie and rot on a dungeon floor.

She breathed darkness, watching it invade and inflate the cooling body. The corpse clambered to its feet. It stared, eyes blank, lips slack and drooling.

"Much better," she said. "See? I'm not such a bad person, for a necromancer."

She smiled.

"When more come you'll have lots of friends."

Dormant
S.O. Green

The voice called Qash to the Tomb of the Lich King.

"Power awaits."

He didn't cast a single spell as he descended into the crypt. The guardians were long-dead, the magic dormant, and even the traps were corroded with age.

Useless.

"As promised."

All that remained was to take the amulet, still pulsing with the sorcerer's terrible magic. He could feel its power. Hear it whispering.

"Your reward."

Qash knew he was worthy to be its master. He fastened the chain around his neck, and heard the Lich King's laughter echoing in his mind.

"Yes. Your body will do nicely."

Hear the Ocean
S.O. Green

"If you listen to seashells, you can hear the ocean."

"We're already at the ocean."

Gail waved at the stretch of blue spanning to the horizon. Salt and seafoam. Fran shrugged, then held a conch to her ear.

What did she expect, trying to make friends with the weird girl in town? This was fun to Fran.

They sat with their shells for hours, until Gail's eyes turned dark and her face went slack. The sea worked its magic.

"You can hear it, can't you?" Fran asked.

Gail nodded. "What do I...?"

"Bring someone else," she said. "Bring them all."

S.O. Green

Simone Oldman Green is a genre-fluid writer and editor living in the Kingdom of Fife with husband, John. Author of over 60 published works with 10 different imprints. Writer, vegan, martial artist, gamer, occasionally a terrible person (but only to fictional people).

Website: https://thebasementoflove.blogspot.com/
Facebook: https://www.facebook.com/thebasementoflove
Twitter: https://twitter.com/SOGreenWriter

Ambition
T.M. Brown

A king without a kingdom stands amongst the ruins of a shattered army, his face shadowed and his body crooked. He raises a gnarled staff high overhead, dust stirring in the stagnant air. Ancient bones scrape and rattle as warriors of a bygone age emerge from a restless slumber.

Their heraldry is faded beyond recognition, and their noble houses are long forgotten. Scavengers have claimed their last vestiges of humanity.

Only husks remain.

The Cloistered King smiles. His soldiers will never tire; they will never hunger or thirst, nor waver in the conduct of their lord's command.

They are perfect.

Purpose
T.M. Brown

Rodric no longer strained against his bindings, his body broken. Escape was beyond hope as an Obsidian Acolyte with sharp, predatory features leaned over him.

"They've told you that there is such a thing as dark magic…" She ran a finger along his swollen, dislocated joints. His blood began to boil.

"That," she stated firmly, "is a lie." She placed a finger under Rodric's chin and guided his gaze to meet her's. "There is neither light nor dark…only purpose and futility." The glow of her stained flesh intensified, then the burning followed. "Your resistance…your pain…is without purpose."

Tradition
T.M. Brown

The crone arrived in the wake of a summer storm. Her back was bent and features aged, a bronze amulet dangling from her neck. The farmers of Byron's Ford complied with custom, offering what little they could spare. The crone accepted their hospitality and took up residence in an abandoned woodshed.

Days passed and the visitor lingered. The crops withered and livestock perished, resentment growing amongst the farmers. When they finally set the woodshed ablaze, a young woman emerged—untouched by the flames. She wore a bronze amulet. The visitor thanked her hosts for their generosity, and then consumed them all.

T.M. Brown

T.M. Brown serves as an officer in the U.S. Army. He currently lives in Colorado Springs, Colorado with his beautiful wife, Anna, and his two dogs, Fry and Zapp. Although Trevor has long held a passion for speculative fiction, he has only recently taken up writing for publication. His first novel, The Gloam, will be published by Terror Tract in the autumn of 2020. He also has a variety of dark fiction under contract with publishers including: Black Hare Press, Breaking Rules Publishing, Cosmic Horror Monthly, Eerie River Publishing, Kyanite Press, and Sinister Smile Press.

Hide and Freak
Chris Hewitt

"Hide and seek. Let's go find the freak," chanted the children scattering into the ruins. Tamara ran as fast as her legs would carry her. This time they'd not catch her, not beat her. This time she had her grandmother's wand.

"Come and get me," she taunted her pursuers, pulling them deeper into the old monastery. The gnarled wand tingled in her hand, eager to do her bidding.

"She's here," hollered a boy, bursting into the quadrangle. His friends stood around, frozen, each one a drained cadaver. They crumbled to dust on a breath of wind. Tamara grinned. "Run, freak!"

The Burning
Chris Hewitt

Elin pushed through the baying crowd until she reached the blazing pyre. Her mother had begged her not to come; staring into her cloudy eyes Elin knew why. Her mother's gentle smile was now a tight-lipped, toothy grin. Long, blonde hair became burnt wicks; Elin stifled a scream, biting her hand until she tasted blood.

Unable to watch she ran, cursing the crazed villagers. Collapsing against the town's well she remembered her mother, remembered her lessons, and squeezed her fist tight. Her dark, corrupted blood dripped into its depths.

Come tomorrow the village would get a taste of Elin's anguish.

Bloody Summoners!
Chris Hewitt

"Oi!" cried Zak, his pint spilling. "Bloody summoners."

"You what?" said the conjurer, his monstrous, demonic pet looming nearby.

Zak sighed. He only wanted a quiet drink. "I said, 'Bloody summoners'!"

The inn fell silent, and Zak stared across a packed room of conjurers and their creations.

"Say that again!" said the conjurer, nodding to his threatening companions.

Zak rolled his eyes, revealing dark orbs. Twisting, phantasmal tentacles snaked from his fingers, sucking the life from every minion they touched.

With the inn half empty he wiped his lips, satisfied that he wouldn't be drinking on an empty stomach tonight.

I'll Die on that Hill
Chris Hewitt

Aliyah sat on a pile of corpses watching the fog roll across the battlefield. How many had died today? A thousand? Two thousand? She'd lost count.

"Die, demon," cried another soldier, running through the mist, spear brandished.

She rolled her eyes. "Again? Look about you. Hasn't there been enough death?"

Stumbling over his fallen brethren the warrior snarled. "Damn, you!"

With a *thud* his spear struck Aliyah in her dark heart. She slumped over, seemingly dead, the swirling mists solidifying to choke the soldier. Aliyah gasped, her rattling breath reaping the fool's soul; another withered warrior reunited with his legion.

Seen, But Not Heard
Chris Hewitt

Hector walked in darkness, a shadow of the man he'd been only a moment earlier. His body lay where it'd fallen, bottle still in hand. Eve stood trembling over it.

"I warned you," she spat, kicking his corpse. "Do you hear me now, Father?"

Hector's shadowy fingers curled into fists as he snarled a mute curse and lunged from the gloom. Eve spun around to face him, swollen, bruised cheeks dewy with tears. He froze at the sight of her hate-filled, glowing green eyes.

"Now it's your turn to be seen, but not heard," she said, striding straight through him.

Chris Hewitt

Chris resides in the beautiful garden of England, Kent UK and in the odd moments that he isn't dog walking he pursues his passion for all things horror, fantasy and science-fiction.

Blog: https://mused.blog/
Twitter: @i_mused_blog
Facebook: https://www.facebook.com/chris.hewitt.writer

MORE FROM EERIE RIVER

FORGOTTEN ONES:
DRABBLES OF MYTH AND LEGEND

COMING SOON

IT CALLS FROM THE SEA

Don't Miss Out!

Looking for a FREE BOOK?

Sign up for Eerie River Publishing's monthly newsletter and get Darkness Reclaimed as our thank you gift!

Sign up for our newsletter
https://mailchi.mp/71e45b6d5880/welcomebook

Here at Eerie River Publishing, we are focused on providing paid writing opportunities for all indie authors. Outside of our limited drabble collections we put out each year, every single written piece that we publish -including short stories featured in this collection have been paid for.

Becoming an exclusive Patreon member gives you a chance to be a part of the action as well as giving you creative content every single month, no matter the tier. Free eBooks, monthly short stories and even paperbacks before they are released.

https://www.patreon.com/EerieRiverPub

Printed in Great Britain
by Amazon